HER VAMPIRE ASSASSIN

ERIN ST. CHARLES

MIDNIGHT ROMANCE

HER VAMPIRE ASSASSIN

She saw more than she should...

For more than a millennium, I have roamed the Earth, a lone hunter killing the creatures that murdered my family.

Until a dark-skinned beauty discovers my sacred mission, but proves impervious to my mind-wiping skills.

Turns out the sassy little human has secrets of her own. Secrets that enable my deadly mission. Secrets that put us both in danger.

When I taste her for the first time, there's no going back.

I'm keeping her, and when I'm done with her, I will make her crave my mastery.

I will make her crave my bite.

1

Hermod

I LOVE THE NIGHT.

After centuries of roaming the Earth, what was once my enemy is now my comfort.

There is risk in going about my business in the way I do —risk and danger—but the darkness mitigates it, the dark shadows punctuated by the transitory, slanting light that passes over the hood of my charcoal gray Pontiac GTO as I pursue my prey.

The darkness obscures the risk.

My prey stops at a convenience store just a few blocks from Club Toxic—where I hold my "day" job, so to speak— and I halt as well, stopping a discreet distance away, extinguishing my lights. I wonder what on earth someone— some*thing*—like this prey could possibly need from a convenience store. It's not like the local 7-Eleven carries the sort of food these creatures need to survive. Is it picking up cigarettes? I smile at the thought of a Marlboro dangling from the side of a mouth filled with rows and rows of razor-sharp teeth. I imagine it extending a withered claw tipped by long, black talons, to tap the ash gathering at the glowing tip of the cigarette.

The street is lit with clubs and bars, places to which humans flock to enjoy themselves. The streets are not crowded as they might be when it is summer and the weather is warmer, but there are clusters of humans here and there, lined up to enter one of the clubs, walking briskly from place to place. I hear the tinkle of distant, drunken laughter, and figure I need to be as quiet as I possibly can be. If push comes to shove, I can deal with any witnesses to me putting down my prey, but it's always best to avoid potential loose ends.

Like the rest of its kind, I expect my prey will be hard to kill. Bullets and knives cannot penetrate the deceptively thin, gray skin that covers their bodies. From the time the nest that included my sire descended on my village and tried to turn my family, I have trained with the deadliest vampire assassins. I am eleven hundred years old, my sire was nearly as old when he turned me, and I have killed many changelings in my time.

As I look on, the changeling disguised as a human exits the store, and sets off down the block again. Like vampires, changelings are creatures of the night, although they don't turn to ash with the rising sun, they prefer darkness and shadows. I debate whether I should follow my prey on foot, or follow in my car. When I see it go around a corner and disappear from sight, I quickly get out of my car, lock it, and follow the creature, careful to stay a few yards behind it.

Tucson is a desert city, warm during the day, and cool at night. Tonight, the air is still, and the temperature hovers in the forties—pleasant, but I'm aware my footsteps will carry if I'm not careful. The creature looks like any human white male, with dark brown hair that grazes its shoulders, a convincing line of scruff along its jawline, and it's hunched over as if the chill of the night affects it. It wears jeans, a t-shirt with a light sport coat, and cowboy boots. I can see even from this distance that its clothing is expensive.

I turn the corner, following the changeling, and see this dark side street is all but abandoned. But the creature is nearby. I detect the swirling scents of many nearby humans: sweat, arousal, musk, and the rusty smell of human blood. The scents are indistinct, jumbled together, mostly because there's so many of them, and none of them are special. There is also something that smells sweet and flowery. And it smells like fear.

Sweetblood.

I frown, wondering where the scent is coming from. The very delicious, attractive scent. If I had more time...

But the creature is also nearby, close enough that the scent of brimstone and burning, rotting garbage—the trademark scent of changelings—hovers in the night air. Humans cannot scent changelings, which is why the creatures are so dangerous.

I slow my pace, then pause, knowing the changeling must be nearby. It occurs to me then that the street is far darker than it should be, darker than even the late hour would suggest, and I see that the streetlights on this block are all out. With slow, controlled movements, I look left and right, trying to put eyes on the changeling. There's nothing around me but the windless night, and traces of the sweet-smelling human I noticed before. I look up and see the end of a hairless gray tail disappearing over the roof line.

The changeling.

I want to stay and soak in more of that lovely scent, but duty calls.

A moment later, in a blur, I am on top of the building, landing softly to avoid alerting the convenience store clerk to my—our—presence. The changeling, anticipating my move, has scrambled over to the opposite edge of the roof. It shed its human identity, and its clothing flew in all directions. I have always thought changelings resemble a cross between a praying mantis and a gargoyle. It stands there on long, spindly legs, grinning to show off the rows and rows of long, white, pointy teeth, its overlarge irises swirling green and yellow with malice.

"Bloodsucker," it hisses, crouching and flicking its tail. "Why are you following me?"

"You know what I want." I walk toward it slowly. Deliberately. This creature must know I've been tracking its clutch since I moved here six months ago. I have already eliminated three of the nine nest mates. Still, it is full of bravado, thinking it can outrun me. It lashes its tail and hisses at me as I get closer. Despite their frail appearance, changelings are amazingly strong, and vicious fighters to boot.

I blur again, surprising it, and it lets out a shriek, but I grasp it by the neck with one hand, cutting off its air supply and silencing its scream. It thrashes and bucks against me, trying desperately to get free from me. Its eyes bug out and it gasps silently for air.

"I'm going to put you down, just like the other three," I tell the creature. "And then I'm going to kill the rest of you."

The creature registers panic and begins its struggles anew. It claws at the fabric of my dress shirt, and that annoys me, because I like this shirt. So I squeeze harder, until the gray, scaly skin turns purple and its struggles lessen. Still, I hold on, because changelings are good at faking death.

I then become aware that the creature is winding its tail around my midsection like a boa constrictor. This won't do much, because I have no breath to steal, but it does have the effect of knocking me a bit off balance. I squeeze tighter, but so does the changeling, and suddenly, I realize the tail is wrapped around my leg. I no sooner realize this than I'm suddenly off my feet, flung off the roof, landing on my back in the alley behind the convenience store. As I spring to my feet, I feel something land on my shoulders. The tail now snakes around my neck, and squeezes. There isn't much the creature can do to me, except snap my head off my body—which would not end well for me.

Changelings are tough, but they do experience pain, and this one shrieks and screams and claws at me when I back into a brick wall in order to dislodge it. I back up again and again, bashing it against the wall, until I feel the thick tail start to go slack around my neck. I hear bricks crumbling behind me, smell mortar dust, but still I keep backing into the wall, until the creature goes completely slack around me. I slam the changeling to the ground and amid the rotting garbage of nearby dumpsters, keeping steady pressure on its neck. It begins to thrash at me again, and to my surprise, suddenly I'm straddling a nude woman, a small, blonde slip of a woman who flops and bucks underneath me.

A woman who begins to cry piteously. Her lips move soundlessly, and she produces a hissing noise from the back of her throat. Her lips form the words: *help me.*

Straddling her, I keep up the pressure until the creature, in its human disguise, dies. After it takes its last breath, I step back to observe what happens next. Most of the time, there is nothing else to do, as the creatures have the ability to simply dissolve into nothingness. And that is what happens in this case. I watch as the body dissolves into a green mass that bubbles and hisses until there is nothing left of it.

That's when it happens.

A gasp, followed by the seductive scent of the sweet-blood I only vaguely scented before. The scent is stronger, closer than it was, and I turned my head to find the source.

It's a woman, standing at the mouth of the alley, watching me with wide, horrified eyes. She is wearing black running tights and a long-sleeved t-shirt, along with a base-ball cap with an Arizona Coyotes logo on the front. Her skin is smooth, unblemished, and the color of a pecan shell. Her mouth forms an O of astonishment and as I walk towards her, there is only a moment's hesitation as she looks me up and down.

She holds a mobile phone in one hand, looking between it and me.

Then she runs.

2

Luna

Did I just see that?

Men do not just come flying off roofs, pick themselves up as if nothing had happened, then strangle creepy insectoid critters to death. Insectoid critters do not turn into naked blonde women, then turn back into insectoids, expire, and dissolve into bubbling, gelatinous masses.

Therefore, I conclude that I'm simply seeing things. Too much time at home alone due to my agoraphobia, with too little human contact, finally has me cracking up. I'm simply losing my mind, that's all there is to it. Still, I run from the scene I'm pretty sure didn't actually happen. I run away from the ruggedly beautiful, strapping blond man; the bubbling mass of goo that was once an insectoid being and blonde woman; the convenience store; and the dark little side street that pinged my psychic prey instinct.

To the right is the wide, well-lit street where small crowds of people bustle by on their way to the clubs that line the avenue. Even thinking about being near all those lights, all those people, makes me nauseous, makes my heart pound wildly against my ribcage. These are the leading signs of a full-fledged panic attack so I do the only thing I can: I run into the darkness.

Adrenaline courses through my blood, urging me away from the unbelievable scene. My feet carry me along the quiet side streets, past the thrift stores; tailors, flower shops and the like, which closed for the evening hours ago, their darkened windows gaping at me, the only witnesses to my flight.

I hear nothing behind me as I run and run, my Nikes pounding the pavement, my heart pounding in my ears, my mind processing the crazed visions of what I just witnessed. Somewhere along the way, I lose my Arizona Coyotes ball cap but I keep my phone, which I had planned to use to call the police—except the blond man spotted me. I need to find a safe place to stop and call the police.

But where?

As I ponder this question, scanning the darkened streets, I feel a flash of wind smack into me, almost as if I've been pushed. I falter, rolling my ankle in the process. I gasp and stumble over my own feet and, like a tree being felled in the forest, begin to fall towards the pavement. I put my hands out to break my fall, already thinking about how this is going to tear up my palms and how much that is going to suck, but something stops my fall. There's a hand around my wrist, firm and solid like a manacle.

I gasp in surprise, and instinctively cast my eyes up, up, up to meet the burning gaze, eyes so cold and pale and mesmerizing that I cannot help but stare into them. I take in the face that goes with the eyes. It is a man; a ruggedly handsome man who puts me in mind of a young Dolph Lundgren. His blond hair, which is tinged with red, is like an nimbus surrounding his head. He is a study in contrasts, rugged yet beautiful. But his lips are thin and cruel, at odds with his almost angelic, dreamy facial features. The man is pretty, but it's a sort of masculine beauty that makes me want to keep looking.

It is definitely the man I saw strangling the blonde woman, who later turned into a puddle of goo.

His expression is placid as he puts me on my feet. I continue to gape at him, but despite the fact I've just seen him murder someone, my fear instinct isn't triggered. I'm not afraid of him.

I have always had a bit of psychic ability. I can sense danger, like a real-world spidey sense, and that is what had me stopping abruptly during my nightly run, craning my head down the darkened street, and looking for the source of the danger. The psychic tingle in my belly intensified the closer I got to the alley behind the convenience store. When the sensation got as hot as I'd ever experienced, I stopped dead in my tracks at the mouth of the alley. I saw nothing that would trigger my psychic senses, but waited to see what would happen anyway.

At first, nothing happened. Then I heard a shriek, and a moment later, a man wearing dark pants and a black shirt hitting the wall, evidently after being thrown off the roof of the store.

The man now holding me up with the kind of strength that shouldn't be possible. He's holding me like I'm a small bag of potatoes, with no effort at all, and he's looking at me like I'm his next meal. He brings me into his body, holding me firmly and staring me down the whole time.

Then he says, "Sweetblood." His voice is a low rumble that vibrates all over my body. His form seems to brand me through our layers of clothes, and I feel a strange pull toward this man.

What would make those cruel lips smile? I think.

"Wh-what?" I say, turned on by this man who has me held captive, also oddly lacking the desire to break free.

This is the man I just witnessed murdering someone.

This is the man I just spent the past five minutes running from like I was being chased by the hounds of hell.

I should be trying to get away, struggling frantically like the weird blonde woman did as he strangled her to death.

"How did you find me, sweet?" he asks, and as more words spill from his lips, I realize he has a bit of a guttural accent. Not only does he look like Dolph Lundgren, he sounds like him too. My pussy clenches on itself. It's starting to ache. I shift on my feet, embarrassed, even though he can't possibly know I'm turned on.

I take a moment to process the question. His eyes demand an answer. His eyes demand the truth.

"You made me tingle," I say. I don't have the will to do anything else. Something about his eyes makes me tell the complete truth.

"What do you mean?" he asks. His reddish blond brows are knit over his pale gray eyes. His lips twist into the cruel beginnings of a smile. Inappropriately, my mind skitters to the idea of his cruel lips doing cruel things to my body. I want to touch that mouth, I want to chew on those lips.

"I sensed danger," I say. He's quite a bit taller than me, and I draw back to get a better look at him. "I knew someone was there. I knew someone was in danger. I wanted to help."

"How were you going to help?" he asks. There is a small eddy of wind that lifts his golden red locks, sweeping his hair over his face, and I want to touch the strands. He is a really attractive man—so attractive that I want to touch him to see whether he's real.

"I have my phone," I find myself saying matter-of-factly while holding up said phone. I'm starting to feel like I'm in a trance. His strange accent and mesmerizing eyes relax me.

"Did you call the police?" he asks. There is wry humor in his eyes, almost like he finds it vaguely adorable that I might have called the police.

"I didn't have a chance," I say. "It all happened so quickly."

I'm not sure why I'm telling him all of this. I don't usually tell people about my psychic gifts. Most people don't believe me, anyway.

"What's your name, sweet?" He raises a hand and places it on my shoulder, and I realize his shirt is in tatters. He's very calm, though, and doesn't seem bothered by the state of his clothing.

"Luna," I say.

"You need to forget me, Luna," he says, but his lips don't move. I don't think his lips have moved at all during this weird little conversation. His eyes bore into mine. He's going to touch me, I realize, and the next moment, he skims his thumb over my cheek.

I feel a jolt of electricity from his touch, a jolt that starts in my cheek and radiates from there, down my neck, over my shoulders, down my back, then I feel it travel over my skin in a scorching blaze of heat. The sensation brings on a rush of confused memories.

I see a small village in a land where it is cold, and the sky is black as night. I see a band of twenty or so very tall men running through the village, attacking men, women and children, biting them, silencing their screams by tearing out their throats. Then I'm on my back, staring up at the stars, with different colored lights dancing across the night sky. Blue, purple, and green lights dancing like multicolored flames. I smell salt water, damp earth, and the rusty iron scent of human blood.

I close my eyes, and sleep.

I step away from him, my fingers to my cheek. It feels like I've been branded by his touch. My pulse races from the force of the connection, and my stomach sinks with profound sadness when that connection falters and dies.

"Forget me, Luna," he says again, but this time, the arrogant smirk is gone. He stares into my eyes searchingly, and it is his turn to look confused.

"Hermod," I say his name. "I can't."

Then my world goes black.

3

_____

Hermod

Luna is dead asleep in the back seat of the GTO, her long limbs folded up in the tiny backseat. Her long, curly eyelashes twitch as she dreams. A wedge of yellowish street-lamp light is cast over her deliciously high, plump cheek-bones. Her full lips are parted, and I can smell her sweet breath. She smells like strawberries. I wonder whether she tastes like strawberries, too.

How on earth does this human girl know my name?

The thought races through my mind like a hamster racing on a wheel. I puzzle the problem over, and realize there is only one explanation that makes sense. The unset-tling truth is that Luna has the power to burrow into my mind. She can read my thoughts, see my memories.

Efforts to wipe her were unsuccessful, a situation I have never before encountered.

The only acceptable answer to the command "forget me," is "yes." Luna didn't say yes, and part of me realizes it's because my thrall does not work on her.

I don't like it.

I dislike it so much that I am hard pressed to understand why I haven't yet put down the sweet-smelling Ms. Luna. She witnessed the changeling turn into the more sympathetic guise of a human woman, no doubt as a last-ditch effort to save its own hide. Luna saw me strangle the changeling. She saw it dissolve into nothingness. Not even my nest mates at Club Toxic know about my extracurricular activities of the changeling-slaying nature.

What do I do with her now? I don't know where she lives. I should simply put her down. Kill her, drive her corpse out to the desert, and leave her there for the coyotes. She's a witness—one who could bring me down. One who could bring down the mission I have been devoted to for centuries.

I lean over the backseat and touch her hair, which is styled into many thin, long braids. It is pulled back from her face in a low, loose ponytail.

"You are beautiful," I say.

She moans and stirs in her sleep.

"What am I going to do with you?" I ask her sleeping form.

I start the car, pull away from the curb, and drive. Away from the convenience store. Away from the nightlife. Away from the twinkly lights of the city and its half a million souls.

On the outskirts of town, she begins to wake up. I hear the subtle shift in her breathing. Her heartbeat increases from that of the slow, steady beat of a human deep in sleep. It takes her nearly a minute to come fully to consciousness, but she keeps her eyes closed for several minutes.

Something compels me to pull over at the next rest stop and wait. Outside, the only other vehicle in the rest stop lot is an eighteen wheeler. If I strained my ears, I could hear the thrum of the human hearts beating in the cab of the truck.

Luna does not move. After a few minutes, I realize she intends to continue feigning sleep.

"I know you're awake," I say, looking through the windshield. The only sounds, other than my own voice, are her heartbeats and the sounds of moths hitting the halide street lamps, confusing the artificial lights with the moon.

Luna sighs, clears her throat, and sits up in the backseat of the car. I turn to look at her. She flinches.

"I—" she starts, but I shush her before she can get the rest of her sentence out.

Across the lot, a kerfuffle sounds from the big truck. I hear an elevated female voice, the sound of skin hitting skin, then a female scream. There is only one heartbeat associated with the altercation, and I strain to hear more. The woman's frantic heartbeat is matched by a slow, steady one —one that is so slow, it would match that of someone close to death. My alarm must show in my face, because Luna's eyes go wide and curious.

Changeling.

I am out of the car and across the parking lot before I realize it. I yank open the door of the rig, and see an overweight man in a filthy t-shirt which stretched over his huge belly. His meaty hand is tangled in the long, black hair of a woman whose face is streaked with eye makeup and tears. The man makes eye contact with me. In the gloom, I can see that he is actually a changeling, one with eyeshine that swirls green and yellow with malice and evil.

I have the element of surprise on my side, and I grab the creature by the neck with one hand, and drag it out of the cab of the truck.

It shrieks in surprise, losing the facade of its human disguise. A long, forked tongue falls out of its mouth, slapping against my wrist as it attempts to grip me. I hold it up by the throat, and I'm grateful for my superhuman strength. Changelings are hard to kill.

It shrieks again, and gives up the human disguise, unfurling its tail to wrap around my midsection. It begins to squeeze. If I were human, I would lose my breath and it would be game over. But I'm not human, and I've taken out one of the changeling's clutch already this evening. I intend to take out this one too.

The tail tightens around my waist. I squeeze harder, digging my thumbs into the scaly flesh of the creature's throat. It gasps, and renews its struggles, clawing at me, shredding the sleeve of my coat with its long talons. Its eyes roll back in its head as I cut off its air flow.

"Go back to the hell you came from," I hiss, shaking the creature, waiting for it to expire. I squeeze hard, and gradually, the struggles lessen until it completely gives up the ghost. I drop it to the asphalt, then place my booted foot on its neck to be sure it's dead. Changelings can fake death, and there is only one sure way to ensure they have expired.

When the creature's skin begins to bubble, I step back. As I watch, the bubbling gives way to a hissing sound and the putrid, sulfuric scent of its dissolving body. In less than a minute, the creature is nothing more than a steaming, liquid mass dissolving into the blacktop.

A gasp has me spinning around. There stands Luna, eyes wide, hands over her gaping mouth.

"What are those things?" she gasps. She looks horrified.

I say nothing. I glance at the rig, looking for the woman the changeling had been assaulting. I see nothing, but I do hear the quiet sobs. I approach the vehicle carefully, following the scent of her fear. She cowers against the passenger door, her knees pulled up to her chin. She's a waif, small and delicate, with bronze skin, dark eyes, and rivers of black, wavy hair that announce her Latina heritage.

She's a perfect victim for a changeling: small and vulnerable. She's dressed in a pair of jean shorts, a faded red t-shirt, and a pair of sandals. I suspect the changeling snatched her off a college campus. When her eyes meet mine, they turn into huge saucers of surprise and fear. I hold my hand out to her, and she presses herself into the door.

"Come here," I say, making a come-hither motion with my outstretched hand. Instantly, her face goes blank. I can see the resistance drain out of her body, and her limbs relax. She takes my hand and I help her out of the cab of the truck.

With the girl in my thrall, it is easy to guide her to the GTO. I'll need to put her in the backseat with Luna, and find a place to leave her where she can get the medical attention she needs. She's a very lucky young woman, because it is only by chance that I discovered the changeling. By chance I met Luna, and by chance I found the changeling. I decide not to let my mind settle on the improbability of these two events happening on the same night, and focus instead on the problem of this victim.

I can nudge our meeting out of her mind, but anything more than that could injure her, so she'll probably retain her memory of her run-in with the changeling—but only in its human form.

I settle the girl into the backseat of my car. Luna simply stares at the proceedings.

Impatient, I glare at Luna, who has her hands crossed over her chest.

"Get in the car," I say. I put my hands on the hood and my thumbs drum the surface with impatience.

"No," she says, for some reason.

I blink with astonishment. "Why not?" I cannot remember the last time a person said "no" to me. It simply does not happen.

"What are you? What was that?" she waves a hand

around jerkily, "that thing you killed? Do you run around killing people, or what?"

I purse my lips with impatience. I am an old, old being. Luna's lifetime represents but a tiny fraction of my own. Long after she has shuffled off this mortal coil, my life will go on. She should be looking at me as the powerful being I am. Instead, she is the picture of defiance.

"I'll tell you later," I say, thinking this will finally shut her up. Surely, watching me vanquish two changelings in one evening should inspire some confidence in me. It should be obvious I mean her no harm, especially given the fact that she is, in fact, still alive, when I could just as easily put her down.

"Tell me now," she demands. Her eyebrows are crammed together with the force of her disapproval. "I am *not* getting in that car with you unless you tell me what the hell is going on."

I may have to re-think my decision to leave her alive.

"You'd rather stay here at," I consult my Rolex, "Eleven thirty-two at night? By yourself?"

She just looks at me, cocking an eyebrow. I suppose this means she wants to pretend this is an actual choice. I realize I don't need this aggravation. Let another changeling come along and get her—she seems to be a magnet for the creatures—and have her for a midnight snack. I don't care.

I get in the car and drive away, watching her become smaller and smaller in my rearview mirror as I put distance between us.

A feeling of immense satisfaction fills my chest.

Guess I showed her.

4

Luna

He left me.

He left me!

The demon-killing dude rescued some poor girl who was in the clutches of one of the evil critters, then left me behind when I asked a very reasonable, straightforward question.

As I watch his tail lights disappear, it dawns on me that I'm stuck here at this rest stop. Alone. I rub my arms to keep myself warm. I'm only wearing running pants and a long-sleeved t-shirt, and the desert gets cold at night.

Why would he do that?

More importantly, how am I going to get back home?

I take stock of my surroundings. It's cold, late, and I want to go home, preferably before the sun comes up. I run my hands over my midsection, where I keep my cell phone, strapped to my body by my running belt. It's not there, and it occurs to me that I took it out in order to call the police. Did I drop it? Was it taken when I was unconscious in the back of that dude's car?

It doesn't matter. I don't have it, and I need it. I look around again, as if doing so will cause a solution to materialize. It doesn't.

My eyes land on the big rig. Would there be a phone there? Or a CB? Would I be able to figure out how to make a CB work? Who would I call, anyway?

I approach the rig, carefully avoiding the puddle of goo that used to be the demon trucker. Inside, I find a cell phone, just sitting there on the bench seat. I study it. Should I call for help? Call an Uber? Drive the truck back home?

None of these options seem like a good idea. How do I explain why I'm here at an abandoned rest stop, in an eighteen-wheeler? I giggle to myself when I think of pulling it up to my apartment complex, using a remote to turn on the security system with a chirp, and going into my apartment. I don't see it happening. Just the size of the truck's steering wheel intimidates me.

I'm searching the cab of the truck, my mind running through possible solutions to my predicament, when I hear the distant growl of a muscle car's engine. I wait for the sensation that comes when my prey instinct engages, but it doesn't come. Cautiously, I back out of the cab, and peer around the corner of the trailer to see who it is.

It's *that* guy. That big, blond bastard who slays demons, rescues unfortunates, and... kidnaps joggers like me. I'm wary of him, even though he doesn't trigger my psychic prey instinct. He has yet to explain himself.

He brings the gray GTO to a stop several yards from the trailer and, leaving it to idle, steps out.

"Are you going to play games all night, Luna?" he asks.

Shit! He knows I'm still here!

I don't know what to say, and as I'm thinking of a reasonable response, he speaks again.

"I haven't been gone long enough for you to have found

another way to get out of here," he says. His tone is teasing, and I do not appreciate it. "Why don't you just come out, I'll take you home, and we can both get on with our lives?"

I have to admit, this isn't a bad offer. I don't believe he'd harm me. Sure, being able to kill demons isn't the norm—in fact, there being demons *at all* isn't the norm. But neither is having a psychic instinct that alerts me to impending danger, so who am I to judge?

I come from behind the shadow of the trailer and show myself. He's standing a few yards away from me, roughly equidistant between the trailer and the GTO. He's wearing a black leather jacket, blue jeans, Doc Martens, and a t-shirt with a hammer that has lightning bolts coming out of it.

"What's your name?" I demand. I want to confirm it.

"Hermod," he says. His voice is deep and resonant. I take a tentative step towards him.

"Helmut?" I ask.

"For fuck's sake, why does everyone think my name is Helmut?" He runs a hand through his pretty blond tresses in frustration. His hair is a wheat color, and curls around his shoulders and ears. It is thick and abundant, making me think of an organic shampoo commercial.

His frustration humanizes him, somehow. I inch closer.

"Come here." He beckons me with the crook of his finger. His eyes bore into mine expectantly, but I go no further. Somehow, I get the sense that he expects me to fall into his arms, just because he suggested it. He beckons again. I stay where I am.

"Where's the girl?" I ask, peering at the windshield. The inside of the car is dark.

"I dropped her at a police station," he says. He crosses his arms, and I track the motion. Seeing me do this, he uncrosses them and holds his hands out, palms facing me.

"Did you go in with her?"

He sighs. "No," he admits.

"Why not?" I ask. I catch a chill that causes a shiver to run through my body. I rub my arms again, trying to warm myself up.

"Because I don't do that," he says.

"What do you do?" I ask. I step closer to him when I realize I'm not afraid of him at all. Not at all. I'm only curious. I want to know this man's secrets more than I fear what he can do to me.

His eyes are fierce.

"Tell me," I say. I get closer to him—so close that I'm a few inches away from him. If we were both breathing, our breaths would mingle.

Only...

This man isn't breathing. I should be freaked out by this, but seriously, I'm just curious. He stands there, waiting for me. I get even closer. I place my hand on his chest. Over his heart, which doesn't thrum reassuringly under my palm.

His heart isn't beating. I blink as I process this information.

Then I notice more things about him. His skin is pale in the moonlight—so pale, it almost glows against the darkness of the night. My fingers drift to his face as if they have a mind of their own. His skin is cool to the touch. I move my fingers to the side of his neck, and there's no pulse throbbing underneath to tell me that he's actually alive.

I blink again. This does not compute.

He grabs my hand, encircling my wrist in a vise-like grip. His skin is cool on mine.

"Are you alive?" I ask, even though I already know the answer to my question.

"No," he says. "And yes." His lips curl into a smirk. Then he says, "Are you afraid of me?"

I was before, but I'm not anymore. "Do you want me to be afraid of you?" I ask.

He peers at me. He's an intimidating man. I have personally witnessed him killing two demon-like creatures. Yet, he saved that poor girl, and while he did kidnap me, he hasn't harmed me. He's a large man, and he towers over me.

"Would you rather be feared or loved?" I ask, poking the bear. I should be more terrified than I actually am. This is clearly a dangerous man.

"Neither," he says. "Those who should fear me, shouldn't know me until it's too late. Also, I don't do love, neither giving nor receiving."

His words are clipped, but I detect a hint of emotion in his voice. I get the impression that he does *do love*, he just hasn't for a while.

"What are you?" I ask. "A zombie?"

This conversation is ludicrous. I cannot believe I'm actually asking this man whether he's a supernatural creature. Then again, I have psychic abilities, which is improbable as well.

"Get in the car," he says. "I'll explain everything to you later."

Another thought occurs to me. "You're a vampire!" I blurt, feeling pleased with myself for the no doubt accurate guess.

He sighs and looks annoyed. He starts nudging me towards the car. "Get in the car, please."

When he opens the back door for me to get in, I give him the stink eye and attempt to disengage. He holds fast. "I'm not a child," I inform him with a huff. "I don't sit in the backseat."

The man—the one who doesn't want to be called Helmut—looks exasperated. He closes the back door, opens the passenger side door, and makes a sweeping gesture.

"Would you please get in the car?" he asks with a sigh.

I peer into the passenger seat apprehensively, as if there is any doubt as to whether I'm getting my stranded ass into this vehicle. I get in, close the door, and settle myself, but I do not put on my seatbelt. Not-Helmut walks around the front of the car, gets into the driver's side, closes his door, then turns to glower at me.

"Fasten your seatbelt," he says, looking me up and down.

"Not until you tell me what's going on here," I say, tilting my chin up defiantly.

He sighs. Runs a hand through his hair. "I... hunt changelings," he says.

I take in this new information. "And what are you?"

He thinks. Purses his lips as if coming to a decision. Studies me even more intently, with a glare. "Forget me," he says, an expectant look on his face.

I cock an eyebrow at him, wondering why the hell he thinks simply telling me what to do would somehow make me do it.

"No?" I say as if I'm asking a question.

His hand pauses midway through stroking his hair again. He grabs his hair, pulls it, then says, "For fuck's sake!"

I'm confused. "What?"

"You're supposed to do what I say," he grumbles. "Okay, okay. I'm a vampire."

He abruptly starts the car and peels out of the lot as I digest this startling conformation.

We are on the road for several minutes before this knowledge penetrates my brain deeply enough that I can formulate a question.

"Really, how old are you?" I ask, not really under-standing why this would be my first question.

"I was born in what is now Denmark in about 926 C.E.," he says with a shrug.

I do the math. "You're eleven hundred years old?" I ask. This makes sense, when I think back to the visions I saw when I touched him earlier.

"Thereabouts," is his casual reply.

We are headed back to the city, the lights along the highway casting shadows over the hood of the car. I wonder if he intends to take me home, or what.

"You're an eleven-hundred-year-old vampire," I summarize. "You don't look anywhere near that old."

He glances at me, then verifies. "Eleven hundred years old is the new forty."

I roll my eyes at his lame-ass joke.

As he drives, I mull over this new information. I re-run a highlight reel of our interactions in my mind. The way he got slammed into the brick wall behind the convenience store, then was uninjured enough to chase after me is starting to make sense. The super-human strength he displayed while dispatching the weird demon-creatures fits with the legends I have heard about vampires. The way he was able to control that girl, getting her to drive away with him with nary a peep of protest, also fits. He must have enthralled her. That also explains the strange glares he's been giving me, and his frustration at my defiance to his commands.

"Is that why you keep making googly eyes at me? Are you trying to "glamour" me, like on *True Blood*?" I'm a tad annoyed by the idea that he would do that to me. I do not appreciate it.

"I still don't know why that didn't work," he says, giving me a side eye. "You *are* human, aren't you?"

Well, yeah, I think to myself. Human with a side of psychic ability.

"What else would I be?" I ask.

He says nothing. He pulls off the highway, and we enter the outskirts of town.

"There's something going on with you, I just don't know what it is," he says. "Yet. I don't know what's going on with you yet."

I squint at him, studying his attractive profile. He's a big, blond dude from Denmark.

"You're Danish," I say. "Does that explain your Thor t-shirt?"

His eyes leave the road to glance at me. "Maybe I just like the Marvel Cinematic Universe."

I picture a vampire not having much of a sense of humor. I think of them as being the brooding types. And mysterious. This guy is funny. Or, at least, he thinks he is.

"Say your name again?" I ask.

"Hermod," he says, without turning to look at me.

"Her-mod," I repeat.

"Better," he approves.

"I like it," I inform him.

"I'm thrilled," he deadpans.

"Are you allergic to garlic?" I ask.

"No," he says.

"What about holy water?"

"That's a myth," he says. "Holy water is just plain water that has been blessed by a priest. That doesn't give it any special properties."

That actually makes sense to me.

"Sunlight?" I ask.

He narrows his eyes at me, and shifts uncomfortably in his seat. "Definitely need to stay out of the sun."

"Can you turn into a bat?" I ask.

He looks at me like I'm nuts. "Why would I want to do that?"

"In case you have to get away quickly," I say. "You know,

you're in a fight to the death, and you need to get away quickly."

"Do I look like someone who runs away from fights?" He looks affronted.

I study him intently. Well, no, he doesn't seem like someone who runs from fights, but that doesn't mean he wouldn't run into a serious opponent at some point.

"What were those demons you were fighting?" I ask.

"They're called changelings," he says. "They usually live underground, but they emerge to feed every few years. There's a nest of them here in Tucson."

"They feed.... on what?" I'm almost afraid to ask.

"They hunt humans," he says. "And I hunt them."

This is startling news. It makes sense now why I was drawn to the dark little side street where Hermod and the changeling were fighting. My psychic prey instinct led me there. What's more, I suspect my instinct is what prevents Hermod's "glamour" from working on me.

"I thought your kind hunts humans, too," I say. For the first time, I realize I may be in danger.

"We don't need to hunt humans," he says. "We have plenty who volunteer for us to feed from them."

Okay then. I settle back in my seat. Who would volunteer to be a vampire's feedbag?

"Do you want to eat me?" I ask cautiously. I probably shouldn't ask this, but I seem to lack a brain to mouth filter, and I'm just so nosy.

He looks at me out of the corner of his eye. He purses his mouth, then bites his lower lip. He has fangs—actual goddamn fangs—and their pointy tips sink into his lower lip. It's hella sexy, and I think I understand the appeal of letting a big, sexy dude bite you. A guy like him probably has a whole damn harem of women wanting him to suck on them.

"Um, I'll take that as a yes," I say. My voice sounds weak and thin to my own ears.

We come to a stop not far from where our evening began, a few blocks from the convenience store and narrow, dark street where I saw Hermod take down the changeling who looked like a naked, blonde woman.

"Why are we stopping?" I ask.

"We need to talk," he says.

5

Hermod

"We do?" she asks, her eyes like saucers. She licks her lips nervously. "About what?"

"Quite a few things," I say. I hear her heart rate speed up.

"Like, what kinds of things?" She swallows loudly.

"How you came to be nearby when I took down the changeling," I say. "Why you don't respond to my attempts to enthrall you."

Her face reflects guilt, plain and simple. There is obviously something she's not telling me. It might be something important, or it might not be. All I know is that I have a mission to take out the local clutch of changelings, a task so important that I cannot let anything or anyone stand in my way. Luna is impacting my mission in ways I do not fully understand. I have to get to the bottom of what she knows.

"Maybe I'm just a fluke," she says. "Maybe it's just a coincidence?" The last bit comes out like a question. Almost like she's trying out possible explanations to determine whether I'll go for them.

"I think we both know that's not true," I tell her. It's pretty obvious she isn't coming clean with me.

"Well, can't we talk about this closer to my place?" Her eyebrows go up with her attempt to sell me on the idea.

"The sun will be up soon," I say.

"That's okay!" she says brightly. "I'll give you my number. We can chat tomorrow night!"

"Don't worry. I won't hurt you," I say, mostly meaning it. Luna does not look convinced. "I have your phone, by the way. I can't give it back to you until I understand what's going on with you. And something tells me you won't give up that information easily."

She frowns at me. She resembles a petulant child.

I get out of the car, go around the front of it, and open her door. She has her arms crossed over her chest, her lips forming a pout. We are parked behind Club Toxic, where I have certain privileges for the duration of my stay in Tucson. Ordinarily, I'd take someone like Luna back to my place on the outskirts of town, but dawn will be here soon, and I don't want to run the risk of some random human wandering around my sanctuary while I'm trying to get some shuteye.

"Get out," I insist. She glowers at me. The woman seems to believe that since she's immune to my attempts to enthrall her, I can't force her out of the car. I grab her by the arm and haul her out of her seat.

"Hey!" she squawks. "Let go of me!"

"You should keep your voice down," I say. "We're about to enter a club full of my kind, and they are far less tolerant of bratty humans than I am."

"I'm not going!" she declares.

"If you don't stop putting up a fuss, you're going to attract all kinds of attention I can guarantee you do not want," I say. Luna keeps struggling. Her flesh is warm and firm underneath her long-sleeved t-shirt, and I can feel her trembling. "Inside voice, please."

Despite the fact that she is an impudent little thing, I find myself smiling in amusement at her antics. This girl is a bright spot in my otherwise dreary existence. Defiant and resistant to being tamed, and I'm surprised to find my sexual interest sparked by her struggles. Interesting...

"What is this place?" she demands. Her eyes go to the back door, which is unassumingly labeled, *Employees Only*. When it opens, her struggles cease. She watches in fascination as a huge, burly guy steps through the doorway. He's wearing a beautiful dark suit, expertly tailored to fit his hulking frame like a glove. He stands, imposing, by the door, and generally looks scary as fuck.

The bouncer at the back door studies little Luna, his arms crossed over his chest. She is still wearing her t-shirt, running shoes, and running tights. She is plainly not dressed for club fun, but visitors have come to Club Toxic in far stranger circumstances, and even more incongruously dressed.

"She's with me," I say. When I turn to acknowledge her, her eyes are bigger than saucers. They are more like bowls. "She is my sweetblood," I clarify.

Luna lets her face drop into a carefully neutral expression and I have to give her credit for that, because I'm sure she has no idea what a sweetblood is.

Subdued, Luna follows me into the lower level of the club. We go down the flight of stairs, to the BDSM area. The top level of the club is more for plain vanilla humans, whereas downstairs, our kind likes to play. There's a bar just as there is upstairs, but it's still obvious this is not a typical nightclub. There's a raised platform on which sits Lucius Frangelico, holding a wine goblet and looking bored. It's late, and I have often seen him still awake and presiding over the dungeon when the others in our nest have succumbed to the exhaustion that forces most of our kind to sleep from dawn to dusk.

The room is sparsely populated, it being close to dawn. Nevertheless, Luna's eyes stretch wide at the sight of the St. Andrew's Cross and the spanking benches. Her eyes flutter downward when she spots Lucius looking imposing, as usual. I have mixed feelings about this. Lucius is certainly intimidating to look at, so I can't blame her for being a little frightened of him. However, she never looks at me like that. Once she realized I wouldn't harm her, she became a mouthy little thing. I realize I want her to be a little more deferential to me, and I wonder what exactly I'd have to do to make that happen.

I hustle her to the restrooms, going in and standing outside the stall while she takes care of business.

We arrive in one of the private rooms. Since I'm only temporarily a member of this nest, I don't have a permanent space at Club Toxic, but I do have use of the private rooms, and it looks like I'm in luck. Only one is currently in use.

We enter the small space, which is empty except for a large, tufted sofa in purple velvet, with a high back and deep seats.

"What are we going to do in here?" Luna asks, giving me an intense side-eye. The dark brown eyes looking up at me are deeply suspicious.

"At the moment, nothing but sleeping," I say. "We can talk more about this later. After we get some sleep."

"I'm not tired," she whines.

What happened to the docile creature who wouldn't even look Lucius in the eye?

I sigh with exasperation. As I watch, she lets out a huge yawn and rubs her eyes as a small child would. She is like a headstrong toddler.

"Even if you're not tired, I am," I tell her.

There's a partition on one side of the room, and I move it to the side so that I can reveal the sleep chamber behind it. Luna gasps when she sees it.

"So it's true," she says when she sees the crypt I sleep in.

There is nothing to say to this. However, since I do not want her wandering around the club, I search for the restraints I know are attached to the wall, holding the cuffs up and staring Luna down.

"What are you going to do with those?" she asks, backing away from me.

"What do you think?" I ask.

She looks around the room, finds the door, and heads for it. I'm there and have the cuffs on her wrists before she even knows what's happening.

"Hey!" she says, outraged. The chain that attaches the cuffs to the wall is long enough to allow a degree of comfort, but not enough to allow her to roam around the club at will. Satisfied with this arrangement, I caution her to behave herself.

"I suggest you get comfortable here," I say. "Rest up, because we'll be chatting after I get some rest."

She folds her arms over her chest and looks away.

"In case you decide to get cute, remember that there's a nest of blood-sucking vampires on the other side of that door," I say. "As long as you're in here with me, they won't bother you. If you decide to go exploring, they won't be as hands-off."

She harrumphs and pounds the pillow on the couch to make it more comfortable, then she plops her head down and angrily closes her eyes.

I climb into my crypt, and settle down for a good, long sleep.

6

Hermod

I AWAKE SEVERAL HOURS LATER, refreshed and eager to get to
the bottom of the puzzle that is Luna Reed.

Why is she immune to my attempts to enthrall her? Why
is it so difficult to get her to behave? Why was she out
running at close to midnight? What is it about her that
makes her so compelling?

I push the lid off my temporary crypt and stretch, but
something isn't right. It's Luna. I do not scent or hear her in
the room. Checking the other side of the partition that sepa-
rates the crypt from the rest of the private room, I realize the
couch where I'd specifically told her to stay is empty, save
for the law-enforcement issue chrome-plated handcuffs,
modified with pink fuzz for the comfort of the wearer. The
chain attached to the cuffs and anchored to the wall lies as
slack as a dead snake.

Over the centuries, I've mastered the control of my
heartbeat, in order to avoid the sort of metabolic processes
that lead to premature aging. It's how I've managed to look

so young even as the centuries pass. But upon seeing that Luna has fled, my heart flips in my chest as I consider what may have happened to her. I'm in the main room of the club in a flash, willing my heart to slow the fuck down, unable to rid myself of the conviction that she must have been taken by one of the others in the nest. She smells exceptionally good. Her sugary-sweet smelling blood stirs the kind of bloodlust liable to make a vampire throw out the conventions of civility we all pride ourselves on. The Tucson Club Toxic nest ethically sources its food, but Luna is the kind of woman who'd make a man forget the bags of donor blood in the club's refrigerators in favor of taking a sip of her sweet blood directly from the source.

In the bar area, I see Luna perched on a stool, chatting cosily with an attractive bartender with shoulder-length, dirty blonde hair. She's wearing a deep red velvet catsuit with a dramatic scooped neckline, dangly gold earrings, and black lipstick. I seem to recall her name is Evangeline and she is mated to Adrian, who has been a member of this nest for a few years. I don't know much about her other than her name, and that she recently began to tend the downstairs bar. I approach Luna, not comprehending what could possibly have compelled her to leave the safety of the private room. Particularly when I told her not to.

What's more, they are talking about... me.

"You know, I'm not surprised he would be so standoffish," Luna says. "You wouldn't believe how long it took me to get him to tell me about himself. To tell the truth, I still don't know much about him."

"I'm pretty new myself," Evangeline says. "But your boy has quite the reputation around here."

"I'm sure he does," Luna says. "Are all vampires so bossy?"

Evangeline tilts her head this way and that, indicating she's thinking about the best way to answer. She turns away from Luna and arranges the bottles of top-shelf alcohol. It's barely past dinnertime, most of the nest is still asleep, and the humans who work here have only now begun to trickle in.

I place my hand on the small of her back. She turns to smile at me, and mischief dances in her dark eyes.

"Well hello, sleepyhead!" she says brightly.

"I thought I told you not to leave the room," I say, incredulous. Anything could have happened to her.

"Oh, that," she waves dismissively, "that was never going to work for me. I had to use the ladies' room."

I sit on the barstool next to Luna. She's nursing a drink that looks like...

"Is that a Shirley Temple?" I ask.

Her smile becomes radiant. "Yes!" she says. "I don't like alcohol."

Once again, I find myself expressing myself in a way most of my kind do not. I let out a long sigh. "Were you not concerned about your own safety, wandering around by yourself in a nest of vampires?" I ask.

"You're a vampire, and you didn't harm me," she says. "Besides, you protected me before, when you could have simply left me to fend for myself. And you took that poor girl to the police station after taking down the changeling trucker."

Evangeline whips around at this news, mouth agape. "You didn't tell me about that part!" she says to Luna, her tone equal parts chiding and excited.

I glare at Luna. No one in the nest knows about my changeling-hunting mission, and I don't intend to tell them about it now.

Luna seems not to notice my censorious look, because

she launches into an explanation. "He's a hunter—" she begins.

Evangeline's eyes bug, and she puts her hands up in a gesture of surrender. "Forget I asked," she says in a hurry. She backs away from the bar and turns her attention back to the bottles of booze.

I grab Luna by the elbow and guide her off the barstool, ushering her back into the private room.

With the door closed behind us, I give the woman a piece of my mind.

"What were you thinking?" I snarl, looming over her. I am not above using my superior height to intimidate her. I've been hunting changelings for centuries, and the evil bastards don't exactly abide by the Geneva Convention when it comes to warfare.

She puts her hands on her hips. "I was thinking I had to pee," she says.

"I let you pee before we went to bed," I point out.

"I can tell you've never lived with a woman before, have you?" she asks. "It's a scientific fact that women pee way more often than men."

All I can do is look at her and remind myself that I brought her into this situation. I haven't been with a woman since the day changeling hordes invaded my village and killed everyone I ever cared about. Since then, I haven't wanted companionship in any shape or form. I should have let this woman go on her way after she spotted me with the changeling. Who would she have told about the encounter? Definitely not anyone who would believe her.

But she's been in the lower level of Club Toxic, and the time to cut her loose was yesterday. As long was the woman is here, I might as well get whatever information from her that I can.

"Why did you happen upon me last night? What made you walk down that dark little street?" I ask.

Her smile falters. She frowns.

"What do you mean?" she asks, looking away. She looks cagey, and I am suspicious.

"Exactly what I said," I say, watching her carefully for any indication of what she's hiding. One of the interesting things about being 1100 years old is that you get a sense of when someone isn't telling you something. I cross the room with purposeful strides, sit on the purple velvet tufted sofa, and deliberately manspread in order to distract her. She stands next to the closed door, arms crossed over her chest, expression determined. Although I am unable to hold her in thrall, I have other ways to cajole her into spilling her guts.

We stare at each other for long moments, until her eyes pivot to my crotch, then up again. I see the movement, and my lips twist into a triumphant smile.

I pat the cushion beside me. "Come sit down next to me," I say. The confidence she'd displayed in the bar falters a bit, and her chin quivers. She inches closer to me.

"Come on," I say. "As you yourself said, I could have harmed you before."

Reluctantly, she crosses the last few feet between the door and the sofa, and sits next to me. But she does not meet my gaze. She looks at her fingers, twisting them in her lap.

We sit there in awkward silence for a few minutes. Eventually, I find myself talking about myself, something I rarely do. I have been part of this nest for several months, and in that time, I have made no friends at Club Toxic, nor have I visited any of the homes of the other nest members. I have been alone so long that I'm not sure how I would go about being with others.

Nevertheless, I find myself telling her about how I came to be doing the work I do.

"A horde of those creatures descended upon my village when I was a young man," I tell her. "My village was destroyed. There were a handful of survivors. We were all in a bad way, when a nest of vampires happened upon us and attempted to save us. I was the only one who survived the process of being turned. My sire..." I pause at the questioning expression in her eyes. "The vampire who turned me is my sire," I explain.

"How do they turn you?" she asks.

Do I tell her about the blood exchanges, the burning fever that takes the human to near death? Do I tell her how few humans survive the process? Do I tell her my mate and I were the last two people in my village to survive almost to the end of the process? Do I tell her I was ultimately the sole survivor?

"It's... a long process," I say. "Too long to go into at the moment."

Her eyes hold a note of sympathy. I suspect she knows I'm holding back something painful, and when her slim, brown hand covers my white one, I realize she sees more into my soul than I probably want her to.

"My sire rescued me," I say. "I stayed with the nest for many years, as they taught me how to hunt changelings. I came to Tucson months ago to hunt changelings. The Danish nest of changeling hunters sends us out to hunt the evil things around the world. Changeling queens lay eggs in a clutch of nine, always. After she lays the eggs, the queen dies. My nest searches for news of mysterious deaths of those who fit the profile of changeling queens. I have killed five hatchlings here in Tucson. You were there for two of my kills. It's too much of a coincidence to truly be a coincidence, little Luna."

She frowns as she processes what I've said.

"I would like to let you go, but I have to know how *you* knew I was fighting the monster," I say, taking in her expression. For the first time since the altercation in the alley behind the convenience store, I see fear in her eyes.

She watches me with distrusting eyes. Cautious eyes. Then she opens her mouth, and tells me everything.

7

Luna

I'M NOT in the habit of telling others about my strange psychic abilities.

The few times I have, I have received a range of reactions. Those who do not believe me regard me with skepticism, accompanied by the sort of hard looks that convey the belief that I am cuckoo for Coco Puffs. Those who believe me are prone to pestering me about exactly how my ability works, seeking skin-to-skin contact, as if doing so will give me windows into their future lives.

But my gift does not work that way. It does not allow me insight into the future, nor expose the secrets of the past. All it does is protect me from danger.

"It's what I call my prey instinct," I tell Hermod. I sit down next to him to tell him my story, but when he shifts his knees in my direction, I get up and begin to pace.

"As far back as I can remember, I have been able to sense impending danger," I say. "When I was little, I had a good friend named Josie Lane. We'd walk home from school together every day, until the day she wanted to take a different way home but I knew somehow it wasn't a good idea, so I didn't go..." I let my voice trail off. A lump of emotion rises in my throat when I think of Josie's disappearance.

"Something happened to your friend?" he asks, with sympathy in his voice and in his eyes.

"Something happened to my friend," I confirm. "I like to keep to myself. It's easier. Except about a year and a half ago, I was headed home from work late one evening and I was mugged. I knew it was coming, but I couldn't get away in time. The guy robbed me, stabbed me, and it was a while before they found me. I wound up in the hospital for two weeks. One of my wounds punctured my kidney, which led to an infection, and I ended up in the hospital for three more weeks. The infection was resistant to treatment."

Hermod watches me intently.

"I was spiking fevers of up to 104 degrees," I said. "I was having hallucinations. One of them involved the man who mugged me. The police were able to figure out who he was, but they hadn't been able to apprehend him."

I take a deep breath and stop pacing. I wrap my arms around myself and mentally prepare myself to tell the rest of my story.

"One morning, after I'd spent a night hallucinating, I managed to get only a little bit of sleep, and I awoke to find one of the items I'd lost in the mugging on my bedside table," I say, thinking of the signet ring that I wore on a chain around my neck, that had once belonged to my grandfather.

Hermod's face is utterly placid as I tell my story. His expression is even, calm and interested.

"I told the police, and they didn't believe me," I say. "I think the guy—his name is Raymond Decker—just wanted to scare me. I left the hospital, took a job working from home, and avoided going out when I could help it. I was attacked in broad daylight, left for dead behind a dumpster, and no one saw me. Daylight makes me feel vulnerable. Exposed. When I started going out again after a few months of recovery, I only wanted to go out at night."

"What happened to the guy? Raymond Decker?" he asks.

I let out a bitter laugh. "Criminals are not very smart," I say. "They caught him a few months after I got out of the hospital. He's in the Pima County Jail, held without bail. I'm still waiting to hear from the District Attorney about when the trial will be."

"Do you plan to testify?" Hermod asks. He gets to his feet and approaches me slowly.

I shrug. I don't want to talk about this.

"You still haven't explained how you came to be out that late at night," he says. "I'm surprised someone who was mugged would go out alone, at night." He moves closer to me, not touching me, just closer than he was a moment ago.

"There's something about the night that feels comforting," I say. "Maybe it's because I was assaulted in the daylight, but the darkness feels like a comfort."

He nods in acknowledgement.

"I exercise at night," I say. "Something about the mugging has heightened my prey instinct. It's no longer something that is confined to me. I now sense all kinds of danger, and when I run across a crime being committed, I call the police." I shrug. "Do you still have my phone?"

There's a flicker of something across his face. Even if he says "no," I'm sure he has it. I wait for him to respond in the affirmative.

However, he says nothing. Fine, I suppose, because I'm willing to trade.

"If you *did* have my phone, you might want to know that I *might* have something to trade for it," I say.

Hermod's placid expression drops and his brow furrows. "What do you have to trade?"

"First, do you have my phone? I'd really like to get it back," I tell him. "I'm about ready to go home, anyway. Don't worry, I won't tell anyone what you did. No one would believe me, anyway."

"I'm not ready to let you go," he says.

This is not what I want to hear. "Why not?" I say.

"Because I think you're the reason why I tracked and killed two changelings in one night."

I brush past Hermod to sit on the purple velvet couch, because I know exactly what he's getting at. Still, I wait for him to finish his thought. He joins me on the couch, sitting with his legs wide open, and leans forward on his forearms.

"I think your psychic ability makes you able to find the changelings," he says.

"But I was unconscious when you found the second one," I say.

He gives me a pointed look. "I think you somehow influenced me to drive into the rest stop," he says. "I had no notion to drive anywhere in particular when we left the city. I just happened upon the exact place where a changeling was about to feed on a human. I don't think it's a coincidence."

I don't think it is a coincidence, either. However, I don't know what significance to attach to what has happened to us. I suspect what has happened so far is still happening. I accept the fact that Hermod is something that isn't supposed to exist, and he accepts my strange psychic ability with barely a murmur one way or the other.

"I have never been able to influence someone to seek

danger," I say with a shrug. "I don't know what to make of all of this."

He studies my face with knitted brows. Up close, I realize his eyes aren't blue, as I first thought, but a clear, beautiful green. True green, not the hazel green mixed with brown that are much more common in those with green eyes.

"Somehow, we are connected," he says. "Hunting changelings is a sacred duty I have been charged with for many centuries. Never before have I had such an easy time locating them, giving me the ability to dispatch two of them in a single night. I think this is your doing, even though I do not know the mechanism by which it happened."

I notice how his guttural accent, faint but persistent even after a thousand years, asserts itself at interesting times. He seems to be puzzling over the pieces of the mystery presented by the intersections of our lives. I have a sense that there is significance in my presence in Hermod's life, my abilities gifted to me by some force I do not know, but meant to culminate in my being here with him.

"Connected?" is all I can say.

"Yes," he says. "I don't know how, but I'd like to pursue it."

"Pursue it?" I say, realizing that I'm starting to sound like a myna bird. "How do you mean?"

"If I could harness your abilities to help find more changelings, I could take down more of them."

Well, there is a thought. But is this what I want to do?

"It is a noble calling," Hermod says, reading my mind. "Changelings are evil beings. They don't just kill humans. They take their life force first."

This is news. "What do you mean?"

He sighs. "They torture their victims," he says. "They take something from their victims when they inflict pain, some essence we cannot see, and the more the human suffers, the better it is for the changeling."

I blink at him. I think of how it felt to have had similar violence perpetrated on me. I think about the poor girl Hermod rescued at the rest stop on the side of the highway. How many more women suffered a similar fate?

"I don't know anything about hunting," I say. Aside from the jogging I do around my neighborhood, I am not an athletic person.

"You don't need to know anything about hunting," he says. "I can do the hunting. You just have to help me find them."

"I don't think this is for me," I say. His expression remains calm, though I wonder whether he intends to let me go if I say no to his offer.

"What do you do for work?" he asks.

"I'm a DNA researcher," I say.

When he squints with incomprehension, I explain, "I help adoptees look for family members through their DNA. I also help individuals establish paternity going back several generations for inheritance purposes. Sometimes, I do a little skip tracing for bail bondsmen so they don't have to spend time behind a computer screen and can focus on the apprehension part of their work. Basically, it's me and my computer, digging around databases, social media, and so on."

"And you're able to do that from home?" he asks.

"Yes," I tell him. "It's not too demanding, and it pays the bills."

"It sounds like lonely work," he says.

I manage a wan smile. "That's why I like it."

"Well, you can think of looking for changelings as similar to skip tracing," he says.

This is not how I think of hunting monsters. "What do you mean?" I ask.

He leans against the back of the couch, stretching an arm over so that it hovers over my shoulders without touching me. Hermod is a handsome man, with fine, sharp features. His body is large and muscular and exudes vitality, which is at odds with the knowledge that his heart no longer beats.

"A great deal of what I do is simply looking for them," he says. "They tend to gravitate toward professions in which they enjoy a certain amount of anonymity, but have opportunities to meet many transient people. The truck driver at the rest stop is a good example."

His eyes are intent on mine. Something crackles in the air as he leans closer.

"They target people who are alone, too," he says. "People who won't be missed. People like you."

I frown, thinking of Raymond Decker. "Do you think—"

Hermod shakes his head. "If he had been a changeling, he would have taken you away somewhere to torture you and take your essence as you died."

I pull back from him at this cheery pronouncement. It must be a horrible way to die. I weigh the idea of helping Hermod and his cause against returning to the small, safe world I've created for myself.

"I'll think about it," I say. "Meanwhile, I'd like to go home."

8

Hermod

WHEN WE LEAVE the private room after our conversation, the club is no longer empty. There are several nest mates with their consorts or sweetbloods gathered around the bar, chatting with Evangeline, who's doing the usual bartender-flirting thing common among female barkeeps looking for good tips. Her partner, Adrian, sits at the bar with the couples. Wherever Evangeline is, Adrian is sure to be nearby.

There's a couple using one of the spanking benches in the corner. Luna walks in front of me, and I hear her gasp when she sees the woman bound and folded over the bench, the man standing close to her, leather paddle in hand as he delivers swats to her naked ass.

"Thank you, Daddy," says the woman after each swat.

Luna spins around to look at me, mouth hanging open in astonishment. "What the hell?" she sputters.

"Did you not notice the spanking bench on the way in?" I ask with a chuckle.

"Not really," she says. "I was kind of distracted by the

whole *visiting a vampire nest* portion of the evening, so the decor wasn't really on my radar."

"You didn't notice you were entering a dungeon?" I ask.

She shakes her head. "Is this..." she waves a hand around the room, "something you like to do?"

I open my mouth to respond, but she puts a hand up to silence me. "Never mind, I can tell already that this is TMI."

Evangeline, who must have seen the entire exchange, grins and calls out to Luna, "Don't knock it until you try it!"

I open my mouth to speak, and again Luna puts up a silencing hand, this time placing her palm on the center of my chest. My eyes follow the movement, and I find I don't mind her touching me. She snatches her hand back and her eyes dart away.

"You know what, I'm ready to go," she says, looking for the exit. She spots the staircase up to the main level and sets out for it, her heartrate speeding up to a gallop. I follow her up the stairs, but not before Evangeline catches my eye and nods at me.

"Good luck!" she says. Adrian turns to look at what has Evangeline's attention.

"You'd better go get your woman," he says, his lips twisting into a sly smirk.

"She's not my—" I start to say *she's not my woman*, but it doesn't matter. "Never mind."

I stomp up the stairs after Luna, grab her by the elbow, and steer her toward the exit. Soon, we are on our way.

The GTO's engine hums aggressively as we drive away from Club Toxic. Luna sits in the passenger seat, her manner subdued. She's staring out the windshield, nibbling her lower lip pensively. I know she is thinking over what I said to her, as well as what she saw in the club. I believe she will eventually agree to help me. No one who takes it upon herself to seek out people in distress in order to call the police for help would be able to walk away from the opportunity to help potential victims of a vicious serial killer. The longer she resists the idea, the more lives could potentially be lost.

I want more time with her to convince her of the impact she could have, the lives she could save.

With this in mind, I decide not to take her home immediately. On the way to her apartment, I spot an all-night diner not far from the address she gave me. I pull into the parking lot, the nose of the car pointed at the neon sign in the window. I turn to look at Luna, and I'm struck by how beautiful the contours of her face are, highlighted as it is by flashing neon lights. She blinks at me, puzzled.

"What are we doing here?" she asks.

"Getting something to eat," I say.

A slight frown spasms across her face. "I already ate. Evangeline gave me a burger. You should hear what she has to say about you, by the way..."

"Then we can have dessert," I say. "What did Evangeline have to say about me?"

"She didn't have much of anything to say about you," Luna says. "I'm just giving you a hard time. But she did say you use the club as a flop house, and you don't spend any time with the others in the nest." She crosses her arms over her chest and pokes out her bottom lip like a petulant child. "Also, what if I don't want dessert?"

"I'll make you have it anyway," I say. I've had enough of her bratty ways.

She sighs. She unfastens her seat belt, then puts her hand on the door handle and pushes the door open.

"Fine," she huffs, headed for the entrance to the diner. Even though she is out of the car first, I get to the door well before she does and open it for her. She pulls up short and blinks in surprise.

"Do you really have to do that?" she says, looking grumpy. "Sneak up on me?"

"I'm just trying to be the gentleman you deserve," I say, finding it impossible not to grin at her.

"Stop grinning at me," she snaps.

A red-haired, bored looking waitress seats us at a red pleather booth in the corner, with windows looking out on the almost empty parking lot and empty streets. She goes to put menus on the table, but Luna puts up a hand.

"I know what I want," she says, and proceeds to order a vanilla milkshake and a slice of apple pie a la mode.

The waitress cocks an eyebrow at me, and I wave a hand. "I'll share with her," I say, and the waitress, perhaps calculating her tip ahead of time, hustles off with an indifferent snort.

"I know what you're trying to do," Luna says, leaning back in her side of the booth. "I'm going to make up my mind in my own time."

"I know you will," I say. "I'd like to know what your objections are, if you don't mind telling me. You haven't really been explicit."

She rolls her eyes. I decide I will no longer accept her petulant teenage mannerisms.

"I've done nothing but treat you with respect and deference, even going as far as going back to that rest stop to get you after you acted like an absolute brat," I tell her. "Not to mention the fact that you have a gift that would benefit your fellow humans. With all that being said, perhaps you should listen to all I have to say about how you can help, and what I'm willing to do to make this worth your while."

She glares, then attempts to stare me down. The waitress arrives with the dessert, the speedy service no doubt due to the fact that there are so few patrons on a weekday this far after the dinner hour. She tears off the check and slaps it on the table.

"Whenever you're ready," she says brusquely, before swishing away in her orthopedic shoes.

I watch Luna dig into the apple pie with gusto, closing her eyes and humming in rapture after the first bite. I don't know if she's trying to conjure ideas of the sexual acts she might perform on me, but that's where my mind goes anyway. As she gobbles up her dessert, I think about her reaction to Club Toxic's accouterments, and to the woman being spanked just before we left. Luna was surprised, but also... maybe a little turned on.

"I didn't ask you before, but do you have someone at home who might be worried about your being gone overnight?" I ask.

Her big, brown eyes regard me with the look of a doe in the woods, frozen in the face of a predator. "No," she says. "Why do you want to know?"

"I want to know what's keeping you from helping me hunt changelings," I say.

"Well, it seems dangerous," she says. Luna has moved on from her apple pie and is now sucking on her milkshake. "Dangerous and risky. I like my safe life the way it is."

"You of all people should know that it's impossible to live a life completely free of danger," I say. "And don't you put yourself at risk when you go running at night and call the police when you witness a crime?"

"Yes, but I don't go looking for trouble." She has finished most of her milkshake, and has the glass turned bottom-up, trying to get the last of the liquid into her mouth. When she puts the glass down, she has a milkshake mustache covering the entirety of her upper lip.

She looks like a five-year-old who has just finished a

cookies and milk snack, and I run my finger over my own top lip to let her know she has something on her face. She squints at me, then grabs a paper napkin to wipe her mouth clean.

"How old are you?" I ask.

She looks surprised. "Well, that came out of left field," she says.

"It occurred to me I didn't ask you before," I say. Whatever her age is, I'm definitely too old for her, as I'm at least a millennium older.

"I'm thirty," she says, peering into the bottom of the milkshake glass. I don't know how she manages to have such a trim figure if she fills up on burgers, apple pie, and milkshakes.

"That's about what I would have guessed," I say.

"And you're 1100 years old," she says, "And you're right. For vampires, 1100 is the new forty."

"Back to what we were talking about before," I say. "You go out looking for trouble every time you leave your apartment to go for a run, especially at night."

"You might have a point there," she says, waving the milkshake-covered straw at me. "But all I do is call the police with my cell phone—which you have still not given back to me, by the way—and leave the scene. These are humans who are doing violence to other humans. Not otherworldly monster serial killers who take people's souls and don't leave witnesses."

"True, but your involvement wouldn't be all that different than patrolling the streets and calling the cops on people," I tell her. "I don't expect you to take down changelings."

Luna twists the paper napkin with her fingers. Her eyes are focused on the action, she's avoiding eye contact with me.

"I think I'd have to be with you in order to find the danger," she says. "It doesn't work without proximity."

"I would protect you," I tell her. The words come out before I realize I'm going to say them. I'm surprised to realize that I actually want to do it. I not only want to protect her from changelings. I want to protect her from *everything*.

"No offense, and I'm not trying to slam your abilities, but I'd just as soon skip the whole *putting myself in the way of danger* part, and let you handle the monster hunting on your own. I've already been a crime victim, so..."

We get ready to leave. I pay the check at the register, adding a generous tip for the waitress.

When we stop at the address Luna gave me, I park in front. We sit there for long moments, listening to the car tick. Her building is in a decent-enough neighborhood, but probably not a place to visit at night. I'm surprised she feels safe leaving her apartment after dark, so I ask her about it.

"Why do you suppose it doesn't frighten you to go out in your neighborhood at night?" I ask.

She purses her lips thoughtfully. A wrinkle forms on her smooth, brown forehead. "I was attacked in broad daylight," she says with a shrug. "I don't think daylight protects me. Daylight makes me feel exposed."

"Has it occurred to you that there is a reason why we are both night dwellers?" I say.

She averts her eyes.

"It's just a coincidence," she says, but her voice lacks conviction. She shifts in her seat to face me. "I'm not ashamed to say I'm afraid, Hermod. I can't help you with this."

I'm taken aback by her use of my first name, and the honest fear in her eyes.

"I think you're not really over what happened to you," I say. She goes utterly still and her eyes go wider. For all her sass, I think Luna is still a scared little girl. "This could be a way to do something proactive to help others, and reclaim the sense of safety that you lost."

She frowns pensively.

"How much do you make at your job?" I ask. Judging by the way Luna lives, she doesn't make much money. I'm not so sure she cares about material things.

She doesn't answer.

"I could pay you," I say. "A reasonable wage, assuredly more than you're making now. And the nest offers benefits to human staff."

Something flickers in her eyes. "Let me think about it," she says.

"Fair enough," I say.

Luna places her hand on the door. I undo my seatbelt and reach for my own door handle.

"What are you doing?" she says.

"Walking you to your door," I say.

She shakes her head. "I don't need you to do that."

"I insist," I say.

Luna hesitates, then opens her door.

An adobe fence circles the perimeter of the property. She uses a key card to access the gate, and I follow her through a courtyard and through a maze of low-slung buildings. As we pass buildings, a few motion-activated lights blink on. We arrive at her apartment door, a cheap, flat paneled affair that would pop open should anyone over 200 pounds so much as lean on it. I know trying to persuade her to leave this totally inadequate apartment complex would be impossible.

She fishes into her running belt for the key, opens the door and, when it is unlocked, cracks it open only a bit, giving me just a glimpse of the inside of her apartment. There is a light on somewhere inside, probably the light she had on before she went out for her run the night before.

Luna does not invite me in. Since she hasn't invited me in, I cannot enter.

She turns around and, with her back to the door, gives me a forced, tight smile.

"Well, thanks for bringing me home and... everything else," she says.

"Think about what I said," I say. I fish in my back pocket and pull out her phone. I hold it out for her. When she takes it, our fingers brush, and I feel that same spark I felt earlier in the evening. Something flashes over her face at that moment. She frowns and pulls her hand back.

"Thank you," she says. She turns and goes inside, closing the door behind her.

As I walk away from her apartment, a smile curls my lips. I make up my mind that I'll be keeping an eye on Ms. Luna Reed. It's becoming obvious that she means more to me than just someone who can help me find changelings.

I know I'll be back on her doorstep, sooner rather than later, telling her how together, we'll be so much more.

9

Luna

IT'S BEEN two weeks since Hermod left me at my apartment door. I've tried to put the encounter out of my mind, but I find my thoughts gravitating back to him, the time we spent together replaying like a highlight reel in my brain.

I also think about all the time he's spent over the centuries tracking down the praying mantis-like creatures, and killing them. How many has he killed? How many human lives has he saved?

I think about the very existence of vampires and changelings. What other supernatural creatures also exist?

When the sun goes down, and I set off for my run this particular evening, I slide my fingertips over my running belt, where I have taken to carrying the burner phone from the truck when I go out at night.

For the first few days that I had the phone, I kept it on my kitchen table, nestled between the salt and pepper shakers and the paper napkin holder. It is the most low-tech of devices, a black flip phone that isn't even password-protected. It has no text messages or call history. I'm not sure why the changeling/trucker even kept it.

After several days of it parked on my kitchen table, I noticed the battery gradually winding down, and purchased a charger from a convenience store located along one of my usual running routes. Tonight, I feel something in the night—something different than what I am used to. There's a nip in the air, the desert cooling the way it does after sundown, and that nip feels like anticipation. I'm wearing my customary running tights, a long-sleeved t-shirt, and my running belt. Standing in the courtyard in front of my apartment door, I stretch, then I exit the courtyard and step out into the public street. I look both ways, smell the air, and watch as, miles away, lightning streaks across the sky. It is the end of monsoon season, and if we get any rain tonight, it will be sudden, fierce, and fast-moving.

But I still have time to get in a run before it rains.

I roll my neck and shoulders, take a deep breath, and set off. I focus on the sound of my feet hitting the pavement, the way it feels to fill my lungs with the night air, the comfort that comes from running in the dark. My mind goes blank and I let my muscle memory guide me. After a few minutes, I find myself going down a dark side street, just as I did two weeks ago. When I realize what I'm doing, I slow my steps, then come to a complete stop when that familiar queasy feeling settles in the pit of my belly.

My prey instinct takes over. I take out my phone, ready to take a photo or call the cops, and step deeper into the gloom of the side street. I am entering an industrial area. There are low-slung warehouses on both sides of me. The soles of my shoes scrape the rough concrete as I creep forward carefully. I don't see anything. I don't hear anything, but with every step, the nausea makes me double over, bracing my hands on my knees. The sense of dread settles over me like a storm cloud.

I hear the rumble of a distant storm gathering, and another streak of lightning brightens the sky. It illuminates someone a few yards ahead of me on the sidewalk—a man who is about my height, with a stocky build and barrel chested. I squint and frown, not sure that I'm seeing what I believe I'm seeing. He disappears with the flash of light.

He must be the danger I sense.

I don't think I can speak to a 911 operator at the moment because the nausea has squeezed the air out of my lungs. With trembling fingers, I lift my phone to take a photo, hoping the flash will illuminate the figure standing before me.

And it does. When the flash goes off, I catch a glimpse of the man. His skin is scaly and ashen. His eyes have somehow grown into the size of dessert plates and they are a strange color, somewhere between bright yellow and neon green, and the colors *swirl*. I gasp and as the flash fades, he disappears. I try to back away, but stumble over a crack in the sidewalk, and I brace myself to hit the ground hard.

Instead of falling, though, I feel myself go weightless, and what feels like a giant band around my waist makes me expel what little air was still in my lungs. I'm squeezed even further, until I start to see stars, then I'm snatched off my feet and I see actual stars. It's the sky, black but filled with stars, and my vision blurs. I hit the ground hard, painfully, and with bone-rattling force. I hear a blood-curdling shriek that sends shivers down my spine and makes goosebumps rise on my skin.

I can't breathe enough to take in any air, and tears prick the backs of my eyes. Nevertheless, I struggle as best I can, pushing against the belt around my middle. It feels like skin in the way it flexes when I move. Like hard, rough skin. I suddenly have a vision of Hermod fighting the changeling, and how the creature looked as the big Viking strangled it. The changeling had a thick, snakelike tail that flailed around as Hermod fought it.

The creature tightens its tail around my midsection, and lifts me off my feet again, in order to bring me closer. When our faces are only inches apart, it shrieks once more, its face a sneering grimace. It speaks, its voice a slithery whisper.

"Luna Reed," it says. "Time for dinner, Luna Reed."

I let out a weak, strangled cry and feel myself losing consciousness. The world begins to dissolve around me as the black spots in my vision spread and converge. As I pass out, I feel the vise-like grip around my midsection go slack, after which I hit the ground with a hard thud my numb body barely feels.

10

Luna

I AWAKEN IN A FAMILIAR PLACE—THE back seat of Hermod's muscle car—and we are moving. I am stiff and sore and when I try to speak; my voice comes out in a squeak.

"Relax," Hermod says. "We're going back to the club. We'll get you seen to there."

I slump back in the seat, touching my throat gingerly. My ribs hurt like hell whenever I try to breathe. I touch my waist, where my running belt usually is, and find it's gone.

"I have both of your phones," Hermod says casually, as if he's reading my mind. "I take it you got the burner from the trucker's rig? Why didn't you tell me about it before?"

I'm annoyed Hermod discovered the trucker's phone, and try clearing my throat. It hurts, and tears spring to my eyes.

"You know, that's probably how it found you," he tells me matter-of-factly. "Just because it's a burner phone, doesn't mean it can't be used to find you."

I try swallowing again, because I want to fuss at him for the way he is so smugly giving me a hard time. It doesn't matter that he no doubt saved me. It doesn't matter that he's taking me to the club in order to "get me seen to", something I undoubtedly need after almost being strangled to death by the changeling's boa constrictor-like appendage.

"It's not how I found you," he goes on.

I sit up straight and gesticulate wildly at him. The car comes to a stop at a red light, and he turns to study me. His face is somehow prettier than I remember. He is larger than life, his skin pale, with fluorescent street lights casting harsh shadows across his features. He smiles at me, a real smile that is more than just a smirk, a smile that flashes a set of fangs that look as sharp as needles. I find myself recoiling a bit.

He cups his fingers around one ear. "What's that?"

I wave my hands urgently and mumble again.

"How did I find you? Is that what you want to know?" he asks. His sarcasm is back in full force.

"Mmm... mmm!" I reply, holding my throat.

"I found you... because I never stopped following you," he says.

The light changes, and Hermod begins to drive again.

"That's right, I've been keeping an eye on you," he says.

I furrow my brow. How dare he!

"You're important to me, Luna," he says. "I knew you'd need me at some point, and I was right. It would have been better had you told me before that you had the trucker's phone, but I suppose it's good that we know the phone is trackable. One of my nest mates should be able to use it to track the changeling. Changelings have a sort of hive mind, and have the need to maintain school contact with their clutch mates."

I swallow against the sore spot in my throat, and manage to croak, "I'm not going anywhere with you."

"Oh, but you are," he says breezily. "You're in my car, and

you're not getting out. You are definitely going to Club Toxic with me."

Since it hurt so much to say even those few words, I shake my head vehemently rather than attempt to speak again.

"And since the changeling appears to have used the burner phone to find you, I'm going to have Slash use it to find the clutch," Hermod says.

"Who's Slash?" I ask, but because my throat hurts so much and I can't make words in the normal way, it comes out like "Mmm! Mmm?"

"He's kind of our nest's resident fixer," Hermod says. "He can create any identity you want, investigate anything you want to know, make you rich, make you poor…"

He trails off then, although I wouldn't mind knowing more about this "Slash", who sounds like he could teach me a thing or two.

Soon, we arrive at Club Toxic. Hermod parks behind the building, then helps me out of the vehicle. I am not exactly steady on my feet, and find myself leaning against his long, strong body. He pauses, stoops, and sweeps me off my feet and into his arms.

He cradles me in his arms, and I'm struck by how good he smells. Before I met him, I would have expected a vampire to smell like a musty crypt, or something similar. Maybe a pile of wet leaves.

Hermod smells like cedar and, surprisingly, a rusty-smelling kind of musk that is oddly appealing. And sexy. Today, he wears dark wash jeans, and a different superhero t-shirt, one with a v-neck, which exposes a few golden brown chest hairs. The t-shirt is black with a red, white and blue shield with a star in the middle, which stretches across his broad, firm chest. My eyes roam over the strong column of his neck, and the muscles of his shoulders and arms. He seems not to strain at all, and I remember how he beat the shit out of three changelings, which are horribly strong creatures. I feel secure in his arms, even though I have no reason to feel secure. I'm also aware of him as a man. A strong, sexy man.

A strong, sexy man who is taking me, a helpless human female, into the basement of a vampire sex club. If something happens to me—even if anyone knows where I am, there aren't many people who could rescue me from such a situation. I should be freaking out, but I am not. I feel secure in this night walker's arms.

We enter the downstairs area and many pairs of eyes follow us on our way to the private room. He places me gently on the fancy purple velvet sofa, leaves, then returns a few minutes later with an attractive young woman wearing street clothes, but carrying a dark brown leather doctor bag and with a stethoscope draped around her neck. She introduces herself to me as Dr. Kat. I have no idea whether she's human or vampire.

Dr. Kat examines me, pokes and prods me, then gives me painkillers for my bruised ribs. The pain pills are miraculous and my discomfort goes bye-bye in short order, although they also make me as high as a kite. Dr. Kat gives Hermod extensive instructions on the care and feeding of his human captive, and I'm dimly aware that something is wrong with this scenario. Hermod should be taking me home. My drug-addled brain is beginning to understand that he expects to be in my life for quite some time. This realization is not as unsettling as it should be. If I was more with it, I'd be protesting this latest development. However, I am not with it. Or rather, I'm with it enough to be outraged at being managed in such a high-handed way, but not enough to protest the treatment.

In any event, as my mind whirs with outrage, Hermod

thanks Dr. Kat for helping out, sees her to the door, and follows her out. As I recline on the couch, pondering what will happen next, Hermod returns with a hipster-looking dude. He's maybe in his late twenties or early thirties, a shortish white dude with brown messy hair that sticks out like he spends a lot of time pulling at it. His complexion is startlingly pale, the kind of pallor that could either be the result of too much time spent in front of a computer screen, or being a semi-dead, blood-sucking vampire.

"Luna, this is—" Hermod starts to say.

"Slash," I croak, attempting to pull myself into a seated position. Hermod hadn't described the man at all, but I know instinctively that in a club chock full of attractive, larger-than-life vampires, this guy has to be the resident geek.

Slash puts up a staying hand. "Don't bother getting up," he says. "This will only take a few minutes."

The two men pull up a pair of chairs and crowd around me. It turns out Slash wants to know everything about how I came to have the phone. How long I've had it, whether I've tried to use it, etc. I tell him all about it, using pantomime and writing on a small white dry erase board more often than I attempt to use my voice.

Slash holds the cheap flip phone in his left hand. He flips it open, peers at the screen, and scrolls through the functions of it, no doubt realizing—as I did—that the phone appears to not have been used.

"Why did he have it?" I whisper. The drugs are really kicking in now, and while my voice sounds strained and thready to my own ears, the ache is now dull and distant, the drugs make the pain seem... irrelevant.

Slash exchanges a look with Hermod, then cuts his eyes back to me. I know this look. It's the *how much can we talk about in front of her* look that is, frankly, a little insulting given my current predicament.

"That thing tried to kill me," I rasp, my eyes darting between the two men. "I think I have a right to know."

I'm aware that I sound like a movie character right now. I'm the reluctant witness trying to determine what my interrogators know before revealing what I know. Slash and Hermod study me for long moments. No one says anything.

"You might as well tell me," I say to both of them. Then, to Hermod, "You know you can't glamour me like they do in *True Blood*."

Slash looks between me and Hermod, then his face splits into a smile. "You got a live one here, don't you, Harry?"

Hermod glares at Slash, gets up from his seat, and paces as he drags a hand through his pretty blond hair.

"Harry?" I ask. Because of the lovely narcotics, my speech is compromised, my words coming out slow, like someone wading through a river of molasses. I smile at the revelation of my blond captor's nickname, because Hermod is far too badass to be called Harry.

Hermod rolls his eyes. "Look, just ask your questions, okay?"

Slash sobers, the grin wilting into a somber expression. He studies me. He seems to be weighing what to say next. Finally, he speaks.

"The burner has been modified to emit a subsonic pulse," he says. He flips the phone open and closed, then he hands it to me. I take it with a skeptical side-eye, almost afraid to touch it. Like Slash isn't handing me a mere cell phone, but a stick of dynamite. Or a rattlesnake. The cell is cool to the touch, like it's been sitting on a table all this time, and not in this man's hands.

"Are you a vampire, too?" I ask.

Slash blinks, surprised. He squints at me.

"The phone is too cold," I say.

Slash gives me a smile and exposes his fangs. He looks at Hermod. "You'd better keep your eye on this one," he says. "She might be too clever for you."

"She might be a little *too* clever," Hermod observes.

"No such thing as too clever," I say, and Hermod makes a grumpy face. I turn my attention back to Slash. "Can your nest hear the sound? Is it voices?"

"No," he says. "The frequency isn't something we can hear. I'm pretty sure the pulses are a sort of beacon, rather than any specific language. It's how they find each other."

"They?" I ask, looking from Slash to Hermod, who is pacing with agitation.

"Harry here finally came completely clean." Slash chuckles. "We knew he was up to something, but no one in the nest has ever heard of changelings."

I let this information sink in.

"You can use the phone to find the rest of them, can't you?" I ask, leaning forward in anticipation.

I think about the girl at the rest stop. I think about the creature's tail around me, squeezing the air out of my lungs. I realize I'm invested in finding the last six changelings.

"I think so," says Slash. He shrugs. "Probably."

I let this bit of information settle in my mind.

"And you want my help?" I ask. This has to be the only reason why he and Hermod are sharing this information with me.

He shrugs again. "I don't care if you help," he admits. "Harry just told me to have a look at the phone. See what I can figure out."

Hermod stops pacing, folds his arms over his massive chest, and stares at me.

"Thank you," Hermod says to Slash, while looking at

me. His accent is gruff and guttural. I am coming to recognize that Hermod's accent is more *grunty* the crankier he gets. Apparently, my captor is done with Slash's bullshit.

Is he mad at me?

Slash leaves with a promise to get back to Hermod when he knows more about how the burner phones work.

Hermod arranges me to a seated position, like a child arranging a doll for a tea party. He sits next to me, then turns to look me full in the face, his lips pressed together and brow furrowed.

"What reason do you have for not helping me?" he asks.

I ponder the question for a moment, frowning. "I'm afraid," I say in a croak. It's the God's honest truth. I *am* afraid. I barely survived my encounter with the changeling.

He nods in understanding. "But I rescued you," he points out. "If you joined me, you wouldn't have to wonder whether I would be there to save you."

"Or, I could just stay inside," I say.

"Where's the fun in that?" He manages a crooked smile.

"Who says life has to be fun?"

He chuckles. "After your attack, is that what you did? You stayed at home?" he asks.

Something inside me clenches, and my stomach bottoms out. Most people are too circumspect to come right out and ask me about my life behind my front door, and I'm not sure how to respond.

"I had groceries delivered," I say. "And I have a stationary bike for exercise. For a while, my friends and family took to visiting me in my apartment."

"They stopped?" he asks.

"People don't know what to do with the agoraphobic," I say. I start to pick at my cuticles. "My parents went back to Phoenix. My old friends basically stopped being friends, and started being people who checked in on me."

"You're agoraphobic?" he asks.

"Yes and no," I say slowly. "I don't like being outside during the day," I say. "It makes me feel—"

He silences me with a finger on my lips. "Exposed?" he says. He leans in close to me, his face filling my field of vision.

I nod.

"Then that is something we have in common," he says. He leans in even closer, until our lips are a hair's breadth apart. Everything about him feels overpowering at the moment.

"Is that right?" I ask. "Are you afraid of the daylight?"

"Not afraid," he says. "More like allergic."

"Do you really drink human blood?" I ask. "If so, where do you get it? And do you want to drink *my* blood?"

"Yes, I do. It's ethically sourced from volunteers and blood banks, and yours certainly does smell good."

I lean away from him to study his face. I had so far not had any inkling that he wants to eat me, or drink my blood.

I open my mouth to say more, but I don't get a chance, because Hermod touches my lips with his. The kiss isn't tentative so much as it is experimental. Like he's looking to see how I react before he gives me more of himself. He lifts me onto his lap, and I do not resist. His arms go around me and he holds me gently. I am struck by the contrasts between us. I am bruised and tender. He is strong and protective. He kisses me and holds me close, and I close my eyes to better enjoy the sensation. All thoughts about his lack of body heat and the fact that his heart does not beat somehow do not seem important in the moment, because at the end of the day, he's a man and I am a woman.

"You need to be my partner," he says. His voice rumbles from deep in his chest. I start to lift my head, to feebly, painfully, push myself away from him, even though I want to stay right here in his arms. He holds me still. He starts nuzzling my neck, which conjures images of him puncturing my jugular with his needle-sharp fangs. Weirdly, this is an arousing image, not a distressing one.

"Let me take care of you," he goes on. "Let me help you take back the power you lost when you were attacked. Help me find these changelings so they can't hurt anyone else."

I think about how the changeling said my name.

Luna Reed... Time for dinner, Luna Reed.

I remember the way the creature wound its tail around my midsection, squeezing the air out of me, stoking my fear and panic. It didn't take a lot of imagination to know the savage creature would be eating me for dinner. I should be bristling at Hermod's low-key bossiness, his guilt trips, his too-logical reasoning to join him in his mission.

Instead, I'm starting to accept the inevitability of our partnership.

"I'm still afraid," I say, my mind full of the many ways in which my life is about to change.

"What are you afraid of?" he asks, stroking my back.

What should I say? I know I could say that I'm concerned about one of the creatures capturing me, and feasting on my fear. But that has already happened to me, and I survived it. Rather, my fear is of a more personal nature. I'm afraid of getting too close to the man who's holding me in his arms.

"It doesn't matter," I say. "I'll get over it."

I'm not sure this is the truth, or even if it is possible to get over falling for a man like this, but it's too late to walk away now.

"One day, you will tell me," he says, pulling away from me to study me. "And I will help you get over it."

He leans in and gives me a long, lingering, open-mouthed kiss. He doesn't taste the way I expect. His tongue invades my mouth and, despite my soreness, I strain towards him. Even in this awkward position, I want nothing more than to get close to him.

"You taste like fruit," Hermod tells me. "Strawberries, maybe." He traps my bottom lip between his teeth and sucks on it, runs the tip of his tongue over my lip.

"You taste like honey," I tell him. "Why do you taste like honey?"

He chuckles. "It's mead."

His lips trail the side of my neck. It feels good, and I have the fleeting desire to feel his fangs sink into the flesh on my neck. Startled by this thought, I pull away from him and this time, he lets me.

"I'm tired," I say. When he pulls back to face me, I avert my eyes.

He studies me carefully. I can feel his eyes on me. "You need to get some rest," he says. "When you're healed, your training begins.

11

Hermod

MANY OF THE vampire nests around the world maintain ownership of one of several worldwide real estate timeshares. Though my home nest is in Sønderborg, a small, ancient town near the southern border of Denmark, I am renting a large house in the Finisterra neighborhood of Tucson. The timeshare also gives me temporary nest privileges at Club Toxic, where, if the mood were to strike me, I could play in the club's dungeon with a willing submissive.

Leasing the property does not come cheap, but there is a certain security in knowing that the home I'm staying in is equipped to handle the special needs of my kind. The six-bedroom, 7000 square-foot home is equipped with window shades that automatically close when the sun comes up, and open at sundown. The shades are made of a material that makes it appear to passersby that the windows aren't shaded at all. Inside, it's as dark and secure as a tomb, and I am free to roam the house at all hours.

This is where I take Luna to convalesce after her attack. I set her up in the guest bedroom furthest away from my underground crypt, but only steps away from the nominal master bedroom. While I rest during the day, she is free to work or relax. From her bedroom windows, she is able to gaze out at the surrounding desert. I have an after-hours housekeeper who stops by twice a week.

If Luna was surprised to find I had a house, she didn't show it. She's taken the whole situation in stride, and has adapted well to the confinement.

As a rule, I avoid spending much time with Luna. The kiss we shared the night of her attack has not been repeated. I need her psychic skills, at least until I've tracked down the last few members of the Tucson changeling clutch. After I have killed them, I'll be on my way to the next city, the next rented house, the next temporary nest, the next clutch of nine evil, vicious bastards. Luna is a recluse, and I don't think she will want to come along for the monster-hunting ride.

The other reason why I've decided she's off limits is that she is too smart-mouthed and too bratty, which is the opposite of what makes a good submissive.

Tonight, after I wake up, I go to the master bedroom, where I shower and dress for the evening in a pair of dark wash jeans, a Shazam t-shirt, and a pair of Doc Martens. We —I—am expecting one of my rare visitors, and I wish to dress for the business at hand. It's possible that after this meeting, Luna and I will be out for the evening.

When I emerge from the master suite, Luna's door is ajar, but the lights are out. When I enter the dining room, expecting to see her there, partaking of her evening meal, she is nowhere to be seen. Frowning, I look for her in the kitchen, the foyer, and the front parlor, only to be stymied.

I wonder whether she's managed to get past the considerable security installed, and escaped. Could one of the changelings have somehow followed us here, and captured her? Neither of these scenarios seems plausible.

"Open shades," I say. It is dusk, and the automatic shades hum quietly to life. Slowly the desert and the twinkling lights of Tucson are revealed beyond the windows of the expansive great room. It is then that I see Luna, sitting in one corner of the plush white sectional, staring intently at the screen of her smartphone. She is wearing her customary leggings and long-sleeved t-shirt, and her hair is pulled up into a giant puff of a bun. Her hair is kinky and abundant, and the puff is about the same size of an infant's head.

Her face is screwed into a moue of distress. I can tell the very moment when she senses me, as she often can, because her body stills before she lifts her gaze to study me. She gets to her feet, crosses the few yards between us and, open mouthed, shows me the screen of her phone.

It's a newscast.

"Divers are working to recover the body of Sharon Dade King," says the young male reporter. He sweeps a hand behind him, indicating a small strip of sand leading to the edge of the man-made Patagonia Lake. "Police say the twenty-six-year-old Tucson native was camping with a group of friends, and stepped away from the campsite to use the public restroom."

There is a cutaway to a young woman, with a caption that includes her name and identifies her as a friend of the poor, departed Sharon. The young lady has the red-rimmed eyes of someone who has been crying. She looks distraught and, frankly, stoned out of her gourd.

"We heard screaming," the woman says. "Sharon called out to us, begging for help. At first, we thought it was a joke, but she kept at it. I got up to see what was the matter, and all that was left of her was her... bloody shoes."

Luna's eyes are round with worry. "Do you think it was one of them?"

Yes, definitely, I think. "Hard to know for sure," I say.

Luna squints at me in that way I have come to know means her bullshit detector is blaring.

Before she can call me on my shit, the doorbell chimes.

Americans love what they perceive to be the trappings of wealth, so the doorbell is a tedious, drawn out affair comprised of many tones that, together, suggest the bridge of some old song.

"Is that the doorbell?" Luna asks, her eyes round. She's giving off a scent I have come to know as apprehension. Not fear, just a recognition of something unknown. It is a bitter scent that reminds me of burning chemicals.

"Yes, we—I—am expecting a guest this evening," I say.

When I open the ridiculously large, carved wood doors, Slash is on the other side, carrying a small black bag.

Luna frowns at him. I hadn't mentioned Slash's impending visit, and she is puzzled that he is there.

"Come in, Slash," I say, sweeping a hand to usher him in. "Luna, Slash has been working on the burner phone. He thinks he can use it to locate the rest of the clutch of changelings."

"Right," she says, and follows us to the dining room where a large, ornately carved mesquite table dominates the space. Slash places the small bag on the table, unzips it, and lays out the contents. There is a space-gray iPad, as well as the burner phone, encased in what appears to be a clear Lucite box.

Slash picks up the box and gives it a shake. "Harry, first off, I gotta tell you, do not open this box unless you are ready to fight one of these creatures," he says.

I pull up short at the use of the "Harry" nickname, and

glare at the short little man. Luna looks between the two of us, and purses her lips in amusement.

"Do you mind getting to the point?" I say.

"Okay," Slash says. "I was able to figure out that the phones all have a subsonic emitter that allows them to sync to each other. That, in turn, allows them to locate one another."

"Is that one still active?" Luna asks. Inside the Lucite box, a tiny light blue light blinks, indicating, I suppose, that the device is still on.

Slash grins. "Yes, yes it is," he says. He sounds like a nutty professor, newly escaped from his lab in an undisclosed location. He's poking around in the side pocket of his bag, his long, pale fingers fidgety with barely contained excitement.

"Should we be concerned?" I ask, because apparently, Slash is going to make me pry all the fucking information out of him, bit by bit.

He looks up. "Hm? No, no, nothing to worry about."

Luna points at the burner phone. "But—"

"Don't worry," he says with a loose, nonchalant shrug. "The box blocks the soundwaves."

Luna and I exchange looks. My front door isn't being knocked down by insectoid creatures here to feast on fear, so I can only assume the clear box must be working to block the signal.

"Anyway," Slash says. "Here's the key to open the box." He holds up a tiny golden key between his thumb and forefinger. "Don't open it until you're ready to rumble."

Luna holds out her hand. "Give it to me," she says.

Slash gives us sly smiles. He presses the key into her palm. She reaches into the front of her t-shirt, looks straight at me with smile in her eyes and, just when I expect her to maybe take off her shirt, she pulls out a long gold chain. I've seen her wear it before, but I've never seen how long it is, and what is at the end.

She unclasps it, and I see a gold-toned pocket watch about the size of a quarter, and very old, by the look of it, dangling from the end of the chain. She slides the chain out of the loop at the top of the watch and it hits the table top with a clatter. She squints at the key, furrows her brow, and painstakingly threads the chain through the key, drapes the chain around her neck and secures the clasp, then drops the whole works back into the mysterious depths of her t-shirt. Then she smiles at both of us.

Just when I think I am able to ignore the attraction between Luna and myself, she pulls shit like this. Slash is similarly enthralled by the motions, his lips pursed thoughtfully. He's making meaningful eye contact with Luna, and this irritates me even more.

I snap my fingers in front of Slash's face. "Hey!" I bark, and Slash blinks in surprise. Luna smirks like the brat she is.

"Right," he says, snapping out of it. He picks up the iPad and brings up a map of the city and the surrounding area. On the map, there are a number of blinking red lights, and one blue dot in roughly the same location as my house. The dots must be the locations of the other burner phones.

Before Slash can explain what we are seeing, Luna snatches up the iPad, eyes gleaming with excitement. "Is this where the other phones are?"

Slash takes the iPad back from her with that twisted lip expression he's fond of making. He waves a hand at the iPad screen.

"Right," he says again. "As you can see, there are four red dots, in roughly a ring around our current location."

"But they don't know where we are, correct?" Luna says, looking worried. She's fingering the key through the material of her t-shirt. The key is nestled exactly in the valley of her cleavage, and I imagine trailing my index finger down the warm, coppery skin. I imagine working her over with a spiked reflex wheel, using it to find her most sensitive spots. How long would it take to have every nerve ending on her body buzzing? How sweet would her blood taste in such a heightened state?

"Hey, hey!" Slash snaps his fingers in front of my face. "You with us?" He is smirking at me, and so is Luna.

"Yeah," I say. "Red dots in a circle."

Slash gives me a disbelieving look. "Can I talk to you?" he says. "In private?"

"Sure," I say, for the first time feeling uncertain about enlisting his help.

He hands the iPad back to Luna and I motion to the front door. We step out into the night, where the desert air is beginning to bite. Slash drives a Mini Cooper (what else?), which is parked in the driveway of the rented house. It's navy blue and has a snazzy white stripe down the hood. He reaches into his jacket pocket and brings out a pack of clove cigarettes, and I can't help but roll my eyes at him.

"Could you be any more..." I wave a dismissive hand at his whole person, "hipster?"

He lights a cigarette, takes a drag, purses his lips, then blows out rings of smoke with great relish.

"What's with you and this girl?" he asks. He nods toward the front door. "You banging her?"

"None of your goddamn business," I inform him. "Let's finish this up, if you don't mind."

"Hang on just a minute," he says. "We never discussed payment."

I sigh. "What, you won't just do a nest mate a solid?"

"Nope," he says. He blows more rings of smoke. I'm

beginning to find this hipster effect to be just a little too precious.

"I don't generally go for things that are costly, as a rule," he says. "An ostrich egg, a pet goat, a glass eye—these kinds of things please me."

"A few of your favorite things?" I say.

"Something like that," he agrees amiably.

"Let me think of what I can give you that you can't get by yourself," I say.

"You could invite me to play with you and your little sweetblood," he suggests.

In an instant, I have closed the several feet of distance faster than Slash can blink. I pick him up by the throat, and lift him into the air.

"She is not to be toyed with," I snarl. He drops the cigarette, but the smile never leaves his lips. I tighten my grip. I toss him away, but he manages to anticipate my moves and lands on his feet. Like a house cat.

"And if you've been toying with me, you need to stop," I say, rolling my shoulders and neck.

He puts his hands up in a sign of surrender. The irritating grin, which had faltered as he regained his footing, is back in full force.

"Lighten up, Harry," he says, showing me his fangs with his shit-eating grin. I am a hair's breadth away from grabbing him up by his throat to see how long I'd need to crush his neck and cause his head to pop off his body. I stand there, staring the little hipster fool down, trying to settle my anger, my hands clenching and unclenching.

When the door opens suddenly, we both jump and see Luna standing in the doorway, the iPad's screen lighting up the beautiful contours of her face.

"Hey, Slash, what does it mean when all the dots come

together?" She holds up the iPad so that we can see the screen.

She's trembling with excitement, and her eyes are full of wonder, because surely she knows what it means. What happened to the frightened girl I brought to Club Toxic, and who refused to be a part of my mission?

I have no fucking clue.

12

Luna

WHEN I STEP out of the giant house to find the two not-exactly-alive guys in battle stances, looking like they want to beat the shit out of each other, I hastily share my map discovery with them in order to end the stare-down. The three of us gaze at the iPad screen with keen interest for several minutes, poking at it like a trio of curious chimpanzees. Hermod announces our next steps.

"Luna, get in the car," he says. "We don't have time to waste."

"Excuse me," I say. "I need to get ready first."

He crosses his arms over his massive chest. "Get ready for what?" he says. "We're going to hunt and kill changelings. This isn't the junior prom."

"Just wait right here," I say. "I'll be ready in a jiffy."

Hermod sighs and runs a hand through his hair. He often wears his golden locks in a Samurai man-bun, but tonight, it's free-flowing around his shoulders. He looks like a Viking warrior from central casting—if you ignore the *Shazam* t-shirt.

Smiling and fairly bursting with excitement, I re-enter the house and take the stairs up to my room two at a time. I grab my fanny pack, throw on a lightweight jacket as a defense against the desert chill, and consider my footwear options.

I have a pair of Doc Martens. Hermod has a pair he wears all the time, and they are butch and make him look like a tough customer. I'd like to look like a tough customer too, but I don't think a pair of shoes will quite get me there.

None of my many pairs of ballet flats are an option. That leaves my running shoes, which seem too pedestrian for the event, not to mention the fact that they have reflective patches that will do no good to maintain any sort of stealth factor.

I decide on the Doc Martens. Then I decide it would be better to be in all black, so I shed my light-colored t-shirt and shiny running tights, although I do change my bra and underwear to a pink satin set. Not because I'm thinking anyone would be looking at them. Hermod will definitely not be seeing them. He hasn't tried anything more with me since that one kiss two weeks ago. Clearly, he is not interested in me in that way. To be honest, I think he finds me kind of annoying.

Once dressed in assassin all-black, I open the door to my room, then run to the kitchen to grab a one-liter bottle of water, which I'll need on hand in case I get thirsty.

When I turn away from the beverage refrigerator in Hermod's well-appointed kitchen, I run into the broad chest of the Viking assassin himself. I step back and blink at him.

"I said I would be there in a jiffy," I complain. "You couldn't wait?"

"I told you we needed to go," he complains right back. He looks highly annoyed.

"Well, I'm ready." I smile at him.

"Why the fuck do you need a bottle of water?"

"Monster hunting seems like thirsty work," I say. I hold up the bottle. "Gotta stay hydrated."

"Where do you think we're going?" he asks.

"I don't know," I reply. "Somewhere in the desert, presumably."

Feeling pleased with myself, I brush past Hermod and head for the front door. There's a small gust of wind, and when I arrive at the carved wooden double doors, Hermod is standing there, arms crossed over his chest, looking as if he's been waiting five minutes for me to arrive. He's got a shit-eating grin on his lips. I pull up short, surprised. He's done this blurring shit a few times now, and it never fails to bug the shit out of me.

"I really wish you wouldn't do that." I glare as I pass him by.

Outside, Slash has apparently taken off in his hipster-mobile Mini Cooper. I'm sorry he's not going with us. The man takes annoying Hermod—excuse me, *Harry*—to new heights. Slash is like Hermod's annoying little brother, and I quite like that about the too-precious hipster hacker dude.

I get in the GTO with Hermod. He plops the iPad on my lap, and I check it for the status of the red dots. There are only two now, and they are next to each other, near where the map indicates a location that surprises me.

"According to the map, there are two of them at the Reid Park Zoo," I say.

Hermod starts the car and takes it easy on the way out of the subdivision. I want to see how fast this car can go, and note this is a manual transmission, which is usually indica-tive of a speed demon driver. I wonder if Hermod ever takes the car on the highway and opens her up.

"Makes sense," he says. "The zoo is deserted at night, yet still centrally located in order to easily find victims. There won't be as many issues if the neighbors hear victims screaming."

Hermod's pronouncement terrifies me, but I'm also excited by the prospect of a monster-hunting adventure. Perhaps it's only because I've been cooped up in Hermod's palatial home for the past two weeks, but I'm delighted to be outside. I'm afraid of what is to come, but a part of me wants to reclaim some of what I lost when I was mugged.

"When will your prey instinct kick in? How close do you have to be?" he asks. He steers through the city streets, and through the windshield, I watch the shadows move over the hood of the car. The evening is pleasantly cool, and I have my window cracked. When I turn to Hermod to answer him, I'm struck by how his profile is determined, his brow furrowed in concentration, his eyes bright with the thrill of the hunt.

"It depends," I say. I think of how acute my fear instinct was when I encountered Hermod and the changeling on that side street behind the convenience store a month ago. I've never felt anything like it, though I'm not sure I need to tell him this. At least, not yet.

"What does it depend on?" he asks, glancing at me. He looks impatient.

"I'm not sure," I say. "Seems like my gift has changed over time, since I first became aware of it."

"How old were you when that happened?"

"I was pretty young," I say. "Even younger than when Josie Lane disappeared."

"Josie Lane?" Then his memory seems to kick in. "Your friend who disappeared when you were walking home from school, isn't that right?"

I nod. "It got stronger when I went through puberty," I tell him.

"I can imagine how that would happen."

"The fact is, it's not exactly predictable," I say. "There are probably a lot of aspects of my abilities that I don't know much about."

Hermod's large, graceful hands are firm on the steering wheel, his thumbs tapping the twelve o'clock position as he bites his full lower lip. He slides his blue-eyed gaze in my direction and cocks an eyebrow.

"For example, I didn't know my ability makes me impervious to your attempts to 'glamour' me," I say. I feel kind of superior about this fact.

"That is not an official vampire term," he says. "Don't get your knowledge of vampire lore from *True Blood*."

"Why not? As far as I can tell, a lot of what appears in vampire fiction is actually true."

Hermod scoffs.

"Did you, or did you not, glamour that girl at the truck stop?" I ask.

"We don't call it that," he says. "We generally call it *thrall*."

"Thrall," I repeat. "Well, whatever it is, that shit doesn't work on me." This knowledge makes me smug.

We have come to a stoplight, and as we wait for the green light, I take the opportunity to ask a few questions.

"Are you allergic to garlic?" I ask.

He rolls his eyes at me. "No."

"Are you allergic to religious symbols?"

He scoffs at that. "They are just symbols," he says. "None of which have any inherent power."

"Can you fly?" I think of how Hermod had been tossed around by the changeling the night we met.

"It's more like a hover," he concedes with a shrug.

"When you brought me to my apartment, you didn't come in," I say. "Is it because I didn't invite you?"

He purses his lips at me, then twists them to the side. He narrows his eyes.

"That *is* the reason why!" I exclaim smugly. "As bossy as you are, I cannot imagine you not just making yourself at home in my apartment."

"Maybe I didn't want to come into the little hovel you call an apartment," he hedges, eyes glinting with amusement. "You've seen my pad, haven't you?"

I'm not going to be deterred by his questionable humor. "You won't come in my apartment, but you will sleep in a coffin all night," I point out.

"I don't sleep in a coffin," he scoffs again.

"Coffin, crypt, whatever," I say. "Just answer the question, please."

"It's true we do not go where we are not explicitly invited," he says.

"I think it's true you *cannot* go where you are not explicitly invited."

The light turns green and he puts the car in gear. We drive a couple more miles of city streets and, at last, we are close to the zoo. The iPad screen shows the two red dots are still there. They must be doing something that is time-consuming, since they haven't moved in the fifteen minutes or so it has taken for us to get here. Hermod turns the car off, turns to look at me.

"You getting anything yet?" he asks.

I shake my head. "Nope."

He takes the iPad and zooms in on the map. We are in the south parking lot, the one farthest away from the zoo entrance. The two red dots are on the other side of the park, in the Asian enclosures.

"Come on," he says. We get out of the car and approach a fence on the far side of the parking lot. It is, of course, locked. I expect him to use his vampire super strength to get us in. Instead, he slips his steel band of an arm around my waist and we basically bounce over the high fence.

When we are back on solid ground again, I blink at him. He starts taking long strides in the direction of where the two red dots had been on the iPad map. I scramble to catch up with him.

"Were you previously invited into the zoo?" I ask, practically running alongside him.

"We're outside," he tells me. "There's no place to invite me in. That restriction really only applies to private homes."

"Interesting," I say.

The park is a strange place to be at night. Without the context of oppressive heat and sunshine—and the press of sweaty visitors—the Reid Park Zoo seems hollowed out. The acacia and Texas bottle trees crowd the walkway and cast voluminous shadows before us. Our booted footsteps are loud in the darkness and quiet, and although I don't have the sinking feeling in my gut that tells me to be afraid, I still feel apprehensive. I can sense something coming.

"How many changelings have you hunted?" I ask.

"Good question," he says. "I've cleared seventy-two cities and towns. Changelings come in clutches of nine eggs, never more, never less. Seventy-two times nine, plus five in Tucson so far—"

I'm adding it up in my head. "653?" I conclude, mind boggled. Had he been thrown around like that every time? "That's a lot of wear and tear on you," I say.

"Vampires are hard to kill," he comments.

It would seem so.

I open my mouth to agree, but he shushes me.

"Can you hear that?" he asks, putting up a hand to stop me. His eyes bore into mine, his expression expectant. He puts a finger to his lips.

I can't hear anything.

I can't *hear* anything, but I can *feel* something.

That "bottom falling out" feeling that comes when a dangerous situation is soon to happen. I swallow hard as my mouth fills with saliva.

Hermod steps forward gingerly, and I follow. We creep towards the sound—and, in my case, my sense of dread— until I am pretty sure I can hear piteous whimpering. Changelings must not have very good hearing, because as we draw nearer to the sounds of distress, we manage to get close to them.

In the pathway running in front of the tiger enclosure are two changelings in what must be their natural forms, circling a small, dark-skinned woman who sits on her haunches, with her legs curled up and her arms clasped tightly around her legs. The woman is letting out low whimpers and rocking in place.

Looks like we found what we came looking for.

13

Hermod

TWO CHANGELINGS ARE in the clearing, shifted into their true forms. With their pale green pallor, scales, and long, muscular tails, they resemble a cross between a praying mantis and a velociraptor. They circle a cowering human woman, clad only in a bloody bra and panties, who has her arms wrapped around her knees and is rocking back and forth. She's not making a sound. She's not even crying.

"What are they doing?" Luna's voice is a stage whisper, and I shush her. Changelings do not have good hearing, but if she's too loud, they will definitely notice us. Instinctively, I place Luna behind me in a protective gesture, but she is nosy and resists me.

The creatures are essentially playing with their food. The more frightened the prey, the tastier the meal. In that way, they are similar to vampires. When our food source experiences pain, they release endorphins that make their blood that much sweeter. For changelings, the food they eat is human fear. The trucker who abducted the young woman he was torturing at the rest stop most likely had had her for days, injuring her but keeping her alive until she had nothing more to give. Changeling victims are usually female, because human women are able to endure far more pain than human males can.

My home nest began to hunt changelings as a way of ensuring our own food source, not unlike how a human farmer will shoot the coyotes preying on his chickens.

Changelings are solitary creatures and usually hunt alone—just as I and the other members of my original nest hunt alone. I have only rarely seen two changelings hunt together, and that is usually a consequence of food shortages. Therefore, this is an unusual occurrence that I'm not sure how to handle. They are tough bastards to kill in the best of circumstances.

"What are you going to do?" Luna whispers, as if I didn't just tell her to shut up.

Truthfully, I don't know. Standing on the sidelines is not an option.

I hear the light thud of someone's footfalls behind me and when I turn around to see who is there, it is none other than Slash, the wee undead hacker I thought I would not see again until I paid him for the work he's done for me. My mouth falls open.

"What are you doing here?" I ask.

He smiles placidly. "I have an Apple Watch," he says in a loud whisper. He holds his wrist out to show me the gadget. "I followed you. I'm here to help."

I have no idea how to handle this situation. My nest is comprised of hunters who, after an apprentice period, are lone hunters. I am a lone hunter. I am not used to having a peanut gallery accompany me on my business.

"Help? With what?"

"With your hunt, of course," he says. He's behaving as if he could actually add anything substantive to this endeavor.

"That's a great idea!" Luna whispers, her face brightening.

I am grateful, once again, that changelings are practically deaf compared to vampires. These two sound like a couple of teenage girls at a sleepover. Soon, they'd be giving each other manicures and charcoal facials, to be followed by episodes of prank calling and writing in slam books. In fact, Slash and Luna seem pretty chummy considering they're relative strangers. I'm not sure I like it.

I look Slash up and down. He is slender and approximately the same height as Luna. He might weigh more than Luna, but I suspect the most exercise he gets is when he presses the buttons on his microwave oven in order to heat up the hot pockets he inexplicably eats while working on hacking projects. Luna at least runs every day, so I'd give her the edge over Slash when it comes to general fitness. Still, he's a vampire, and theoretically *should* have some innate hand-to-hand combat ability.

I sigh and run a hand through my hair. Luna and Slash grin stupidly at one another. And just like that, I wonder whether there might be a spark between the two of them. Luna is an attractive woman. Beautiful, actually. Beautiful, intelligent, and her blood is obviously good enough to eat. Not that I would do that because, for centuries now, I have only partaken of ethically sourced blood. I hunt predators that feast on human pain. I prefer not to be one of those predators.

I regard Slash with narrowed eyes. *He* might be such a predator. He might have invited himself to this hunt in order to groom and/or impress Luna with his fighting prowess. Slash might be cultivating Luna to be his own personal sweetblood. I wouldn't put it past him.

I think of Bela Lugosi in *Dracula*, and try to picture Slash saying "I vant to drink your blood!"

Slash is grinning like a fool at Luna, and she seems taken with him as well. None of that matters, because I saw Luna first. She is off-limits for all pain-inducing blood suckers of the Tucson nest.

"Look, if you want to join me, it's your funeral," I told Slash. "But I won't be saving your ass if you get into a jam."

That said, I study the movements of my opponents, stretch my neck, and roll my shoulders. I've never fought two at the same time, but there's a first time for everything, and I'm confident I will emerge the victor. I blur into the clearing and grab one of the changelings by the throat, squeezing the life out of the horrible creature.

It thrashes its tail, slapping the blacktop path that bisects the space between the animal enclosures. It lets out a high-pitched shriek that sounds, frankly, panicked. I hear the other creature shrieking in sympathy. I'm counting on the fact that changelings are solo hunters and not particularly good at coordinating attacks. The other one snatched up the victim, whose screams grow more distant as the other creature whisks her away to take her somewhere unknown.

The first changeling continues to thrash and shriek. The denizens of the nearby South American primate enclosures contribute to the cacophony of excited, inhuman voices. They shriek and rattle their cages frantically, sensing the violence about to happen, since there is no way they could actually see the confrontation. The changeling I have in my grasp is helplessly struggling against me, but not able to escape me.

"Watch out!" Luna says, her voice high and tense.

I stay focused on the creature in my hands, choking the life out of it as it thrashes and claws at me.

I feel something large and heavy crash into my back. I crane my neck to see what it is, still grasping the dying creature, and I see a thick, scaly member constricting my waist. I imagine Changeling Number Two is used to squeezing the breath out of its victims, and hasn't quite cottoned on to the fact that I have no breath to be squeezed out of me. At most, being suffocated is an inconvenience, because about the only thing that can kill a vampire, other than sunlight, is decapitation. The constricting tail is nowhere near my neck, so therefore, I am not in any immediate danger.

I stagger as I struggle with the two changelings, and wonder what the hell Slash and Luna are doing while I juggle two attackers.

I no sooner have this thought than the tail wound around my waist goes slack. I glance over my shoulder to see that Slash has the second creature in a chokehold, and it occurs to me that the position might actually be a more efficient way to choke a changeling to death.

Once each changeling is subdued, all there is left to do is to continue to subdue the creatures until they expire.

This is what would have happened, had Slash not assumed that the creature's failure to struggle means that he's killed it. Changelings are good at feigning death, their bodies going utterly slack after long minutes of strangulation.

That's what Slash's changeling does. When it goes limp, he assumes it is dead, and drops it in order to assist me. My hands are full, making it difficult to explain to Slash how his move will soon backfire on him. As it turns out, I don't have to, because when he foolishly turns his back on the critter, it hops back to its feet and lashes out with its tail, which is about as prehensile as an octopus tentacle. Instead of wrapping itself around Slash's waist, it wraps itself around his neck.

I have to ignore Slash's predicament, busy as I am with my own creature. He's on his own.

Meanwhile, my changeling is going limp. Instead of letting go, however, I keep up with my manual strangulation. Feeling smug, I make eye contact with Slash, who is furiously clawing at the limb currently strangling him. His face has turned an alarming shade of purple. This is not usual, which must mean he has recently fed and, as a result, has extra blood to spare. If the changeling decides to pop Slash's head off, there won't be much I can do about it.

"Hey! Hey! Over here!" Luna jumps into the clearing, waving her arms dramatically, presumably to distract the creature. I do not understand this. I would expect her to have enough of a sense of self-preservation to hide from danger and let the supernatural beings trying to protect her take down the other supernatural beings who would kill her as soon as they'd look at her.

No. Luna has decided Slash needs her help.

All four supernatural creatures freeze to study the helpless and apparently crazy little human screaming her head off. Luna seems to realize the fatal flaw in her plan when all eyes fall on her. She goes quiet, makes a little finger wave, manages a nervous smile.

The changeling attacking Slash drops his hard-to-kill quarry in favor of the little human who would prove easier to torture, feed on, and kill. It advances on Luna in its praying mantis stance, its meaty tail lashing the ground.

Luna squeaks, spins around, and disappears up the path we used to reach the clearing. The changeling runs after her. I hear a yelp as it grabs her. Slash follows in a blur, and I drop my changeling to join them. Slash is not much of a hunter; I don't trust his ability to protect Luna, to protect what's—

Mine.

I don't trust Slash to protect what's mine. And Luna is mine.

Mine. Mine. Mine.

I don't have time to ponder the implications of this realization when Luna needs rescuing. I blur to where the changeling has her with that tail wrapped around her midsection. The creature is scaling a barrier to the tiger enclosure, with Luna held in his constricting tail. They land on a boulder with a light thud, and with Luna screaming bloody murder. I hover over the barrier and land a few feet away. The changeling lifts its tail and, holding Luna aloft, it shrieks at me, its mouth a round O, its forked tongue trembling and lashing. Its huge eyes appear to be about the size of softballs, and swirl green and sulfuric yellow.

Before I can react, Slash rushes the changeling and manages to knock it off its feet. Now freed, Luna rolls onto her knees, coughing and trying to catch her breath. The changeling is confused. Surprised. It's not expecting one hunter to tackle it, and another one to put his foot on its neck, which is what I do. I grind my heel into the creature's neck, until I feel and hear the satisfying crunch of its bones. It screams and thrashes, and flops around underneath my boot.

Steady pressure applied to the creature's neck for several minutes finally causes it to expire. Soon after, its corpse dissolves into a mass of slimy, gelatinous goo. It will dry up shortly, and then turn into dust. No one knows why they die this way, but it is damn convenient.

Pleased with this outcome, I look for Slash and Luna. They, too, watch in fascination as the creature dies.

I run a hand through my hair, and look around. I don't see the big cats who would normally live in this enclosure, but I can hear all manner of zoo animals, screaming, agitated at the goings on.

"Are you okay?" I ask Luna, who is huddled with Slash, catching her breath. She nods silently.

When I look at Slash in order to stare daggers at him, he says, "I'm fine too." He then makes a show of nonchalantly dusting himself.

I take Luna's hand, then sweep her up into my arms. We climb out of the enclosure and follow the path to the clearing where we first found the pair of changelings. The one I had subdued in the clearing is no longer there. We look for the victim, but there is no trace of her. But we do find the two burner phones we had been tracking, both smashed to pieces.

The iPad we'd been using to track the changelings has been discarded a few yards away, and Luna picks it up now to peer at the screen.

"I don't see the trackers anymore," she says, tilting the screen in order to let me see it. Indeed, there are no red dots scooting along on the map lines on the screen. Slash steps forward and takes the iPad.

"Well, obviously, they destroyed the phones," he says. "I don't know whether they were aware they were being tracked, or if they simply move the trackers from phone to phone as a matter of course." He picks up the phones and pockets them in the back of his jeans.

"We should go," I tell them both.

"Where are we going?" Luna asks. She is eager and ready to go, despite having been attacked by two changelings in as many weeks. The enormous puff of thick, wavy hair she often wears at the crown of her head looks none the worse for wear. However, her black leggings are ripped at the knees, and her black t-shirt is in tatters.

"Back to Club Toxic," I say, waving a hand at Slash. "We can take this clown back to where he belongs, then decide on next steps." I take Luna by the elbow and turn her toward the shadowy path, back the way we came.

"Clown?" he says, scrambling after us. "You wouldn't have been able to find these creatures without me."

"Don't forget you needed saving by a human," I say with a contemptuous tone. "You needed a human to save you."

Luna wrests her arm away from me, and glares at me with arms akimbo. "What's wrong with a friend helping out a friend?" she demands. "And so what if I'm human?" Her face is twisted into a mask of irritation.

"Yeah, what's wrong with that?" Slash puts in. He steps forward to snake an arm around Luna's narrow waist. I body block him before he can complete the motion. He blinks and frowns.

"I've got it," I tell him.

Luna gives me a pointed look.

The three of us leave the zoo, and head for Club Toxic.

14

Luna

HERMOD SIMMERS with agitation on the way to Club Toxic. The muscle in his jaw tics as his hands grip the steering wheel, and he snaps the stick shift as he drives.

My mind relives the evening's events, from the disagreement between Hermod and Slash at Hermod's house, to the tussle with the changeling in the tiger enclosure. When Hermod pulled me to him, I thought for sure he would kiss me, and I was desperate for him to do so. I want him taking my lips between his, sucking, teasing, and I wonder what it would feel like to have him bite my lips, my neck, as he makes love to me.

But other than the kiss we shared a couple of weeks ago, he has expressed zero sexual interest in me. His caveman routine tonight has me seriously confused. I decide to tell him how I feel.

"What's got you so cranky?" I demand.

He drives on, ignoring me.

I shift in my seat, turning my body to face him. "Hey, you

got what you wanted," I say. "I'm here. What's got you so annoyed?"

"I'm not annoyed," he tells me, but I know better.

"Your accent gets stronger when you're emotional," I point out.

He squints at me, rolls his eyes, then trains his gaze back on the road. "I don't have an accent."

"I don't *haff* an *axsent*," I mimic, trying my best to sound like Arnold Schwarzenegger.

"I do not sound like that," he grumbles.

I repeat the last sentence back to him, with the accent exaggerated. He glares. This man glares a lot.

"Also, why were you so mean to Slash?" I ask. "He helped us out." I realize I've said *us*, not *you*.

"He could have got you killed," Hermod says.

"He came to my rescue."

He turns his head so very slowly, and glares at me again. "*I* came to your rescue."

He is being silly. "You both came to my rescue," I say.

"Is that what you call what he did?" he asks, raising his voice. "Slash let you get snatched by the changeling. If he had not been there, you would not have been taken into the tiger house." He waves his hand, looking annoyed.

"You know, for someone who has no heartbeat, and therefore no blood circulation, you sure are worked up," I tell him. "Why are you so angry?"

"Angry? I don't get angry," he says, seething. His thumbs drum the steering wheel in a fast rhythm.

I settle back in my seat, pondering this. Is there some reason why he'd prefer not to be angry, therefore, he ignores the fact that he is, in fact, angry? I side-eye him, contemplating what to say next.

"Do you... like Slash?" Hermod asks suddenly.

"Hm? Yeah, sure," I say absently. "I like him just fine. He

was able to find the changelings, right? That's what we—you —wanted, isn't it?"

Hermod, eyes still on the road, sighs.

"You know, you sigh a lot for someone who does not need to breathe," I point out.

"Would you like to... go out with Slash?" he asks. The words come out slowly. Reluctantly. I'm not at all sure what he means.

In my mind's eye, I conjure an image of Slash. Skinny Slash, with his pale skin, fussy mannerisms, and deep geeki- tude could actually be my type, although it's been years since I had a type. Since the mugging, I haven't had much of a social life, and I've largely decided to ignore this part of my life.

"I'm not really... active that way," I say. "It's not really an important part of my life anymore."

He looks surprised. "You don't date?"

"I prefer to keep to myself," I say. "I avoid leaving my apartment, especially during the day."

"Why not during the day?" he asks.

"The night feels safer to me," I say. "I know it seems counterintuitive, but the night seems safer, somehow."

"Why do you think that is?" he asks.

"I don't know," I say, not wanting to discuss this any further. I look out the passenger window, watching the streets go by in a blur. "How soon until we get to Club Toxic? And what are we doing to do when we get there?"

"I need to do a more comprehensive debrief with Slash," he says the hacker's name with a sneer.

"What do you have against him?" I ask. "He seems like a nice enough guy."

"But you're not attracted to him?" he asks again.

"No," I say, wishing we could stop talking about this.

"What *is* your type?" There is something in Hermod's voice that catches my attention.

"I just told you, I don't really date."

"But when you did date," he presses. "What was your type?"

"Well... intelligence is important," I say. "My last boyfriend was a software engineer."

I think of Finn, the last guy I slept with. He's a short, wiry dude I remember mostly because, in the five months we were together, he only wanted to have sex missionary style. He would come over to "hang out" with beer and frozen pizza, and considered a good weekend one in which we binge-watched shows on Netflix, and/or played World of Warcraft. I'd broken things off with him several months before my mugging. When I was in the hospital, he never came to visit me.

"Slash is intelligent," Hermod says, his voice neutral.

I blink at Hermod. "He is, at that. But he's... you know..."

Hermod's expression turns speculative, his lips pursed thoughtfully. "He's what?"

"Well, he's a vampire," I say. "We're kind of like different species, you know?"

He flexes his long, pale fingers over the steering wheel. "Is that what you think?"

"Well, isn't that the case?"

"Many in the nest have human companions," he says. His words are deliberate. Careful. He's curious about my reaction.

"Really?" I ask. I hadn't considered this. "Like girlfriends and boyfriends, or voluntary food sources?"

"Both."

"Huh," I say, taking this in. "But you don't, do you?"

"No. What makes you say that?"

"You don't seem like you're part of a couple," I say. "You seem pretty solitary."

"Most of my kind are solitary," he tells me.

"Also, you told me you only take ethically sourced blood," I point out. "So you don't need a blood source."

"That's true. It has been years since I took blood from a human source."

"Years?" Hermod is a lot older than me, and what he considers years might not be what I consider years.

"Have you ever heard of the physician Charles Drew?" he asks, studying me.

"Of course," I say. Every Black child in America grows up knowing about the Black physician who was the father of modern blood banks. "My parents insisted I learn Black history."

"Right," he says. "He pioneered blood banking around 1940. That started the age of ethically sourced blood."

"That makes sense. Why don't you have a girlfriend?" I ask, studying his attractive profile. He's a good-looking man, and I find it hard to believe that he wouldn't have offers from women. From what I can see of Club Toxic, there is no shortage of willing females.

I think of the kiss we shared weeks ago. He'd stopped after nibbling at my lips, though I suspect he would have liked to do more. And I would have liked him do more...

"I know you're attracted to me," I say, because hey, I'd do him in a heartbeat. "What's holding you back from putting the moves on me?"

Hermod sighs and, for the first time since I've met him, he looks distinctly uncomfortable. He says nothing.

We pull up to a red light. I study his profile carefully, noting the tic in his jaw.

"Are you grinding your teeth?" I ask.

He purses his lips and glares at me.

I unbuckle my seatbelt, get on my knees, and take his face in my hands. He holds still as I lean in until our faces are less than an inch apart.

"Tell me what's holding you back from making a move on me," I say. His blue eyes are heavy-lidded and his breath is shallow. His lips are parted, and I can just see the points of his needle-sharp fangs.

"Because I think you want me," I tell him. "I think that's why you've been avoiding me."

I touch my forehead to his gently. He smells a little woodsy, a little spicy. I rub our noses together, then lick the outline of his firm lips. I plant a long, lingering kiss on his mouth. He doesn't move at first, doesn't reciprocate for long moments, and I feel a little foolish. I press my hands against his chest, and bring myself closer to him until I'm practically straddling him.

I invade his mouth with my tongue. I want a response from him, I want him to admit he wants me, but the stubborn bastard holds back. Nothing happens at first, but then I feel the sharp edge of his fang and, acting on instinct, I rake my tongue over it until I taste blood.

And then all hell breaks loose.

15

Hermod

I WOULD HAVE BEEN fine with Luna throwing herself at me—even with the intoxicating scent of her feminine arousal—because I am an old, old being, and one of the upsides of age is near-infinite patience, as well as a tendency not to give in to the comforts of the flesh.

But when I taste her sweet, sweet blood, I about lose my mind.

I moan and curse and drag her the rest of the way onto my lap, plunge my fingers into the soft cloud of her hair, and hold her hips in place with my other hand. Her body is soft and warm, and her promised land hovers over my cock, hot and wet. It is so easy to imagine biting her and fucking her at the same time.

Even with me holding her in place, her dark brown eyes hold a challenge, like she's teasing me.

"Do you have any idea what you're doing?" I say, and let out a long string of curses in Old Danish. My voice is harsh and guttural. "You're like a little girl trying on big girl panties, aren't you?"

She appears to be considering this assessment. "I'm just doing what comes naturally," she says.

I believe it. Luna is a brat, an impudent child whose teasing has her crossing a line, a point in time and space that cannot be backed away from. I wonder if there is any upside to telling her she's going too far. But I'm enjoying the teasing, even though we are both playing with fire.

She shifts in my lap, taking her wet heat away from me, and I object, using my free hand to pin her hips in a vise-like grip.

"You know, I've wondered how vampires achieve erections, given their lack of blood flow," says the brat.

I curl my fingers in her hair and tug, and she hisses.

"Your blood is even sweeter than I imagined," I tell her, ignoring her nonsensical ramblings.

She gasps when I tighten my fingers in her hair and grip her hip harder, bringing her body ever closer to mine. I kiss her again, sucking the drops of blood on her tongue as I suck it into my mouth. With her tongue close to my fangs, I graze it and let out a desperate grunt at the explosion of copper and sweetness in my mouth. She is so sweet. Her blood is the sweetest substance I have ever tasted. I tell myself it's because it's the first blood I have tasted direct from the source since Charles Drew pioneered blood banking in the 1940s. Her essence is sweet, her scent intoxicating, her body soft and yielding.

She tries to wrench away from me, but I hold her fast. My hunger has come upon me with the force of a red tsunami, and with her tongue still in my mouth, I nick it once more, shuddering when a gush of hot, sweet blood invades my senses. She screams and moans, and the sounds coming from her throat vibrate against my lips.

"Luna, Luna," I mumble helplessly. It's a good thing I didn't do this with her earlier. I would hardly be able to get anything else done. I drink and drink, and consider that her mouth is also filling with blood, her own blood, and wonder how it feels to her.

"How does it feel to be under my control?" I demand, pulling away from the head-spinning intoxication of her kisses. She splutters in confusion, blood dribbling from the corner of her mouth. She licks at it with the tip of her tongue, and my cock, already hard from this woman and her blood, becomes a steel rod in my trousers.

"Scary," she says. "Exciting. I wonder if you'll leave a bruise."

I bury my nose in the crook of her shoulder and inhale deeply of her dizzying scent. "I will definitely leave a bruise."

Instead of shrinking away, she arches her body into my touch. I hold her to me, let my fangs graze the side of her neck without biting down. I wish to bite her everywhere.

As if she's reading my mind, she says, "Are you going to bite me there?"

"Not yet," I say. "But I will. I will bite you everywhere."

"Oh," she says on a deep shudder. The scent of her arousal intensifies. "Will you tie me up first?"

"Because I suspect you'd be a squirmer, and I'd prefer you hold still, yes."

Her scent is heady, my arousal undeniable, and I want to be somewhere where I can test out just how much this woman will go with my flow. I am not a boy to take home to mother.

There's a loud blare of a horn behind us. We are, after all, stopped at a red light. Though it is late at night, there is still traffic going to and fro. Making out at the crosswalk is probably not a good idea. I let go of Luna, and she settles back into her seat, looking hot and bothered. My tongue catches the corner of my mouth, where a trace of her sweet, sweet blood lingers.

As we drive the rest of the way to Club Toxic, I do a mental debrief of what has just happened. I'm pleased that Slash took his own car back to Club Toxic, because I do not need his peanut-gallery remarks after what just happened between me and Luna.

I'd forgotten just how pain makes a woman's blood sweeter. Luna's blood.

She sits in the passenger seat, a dreamy, faraway look in her eyes. Her lips are slightly curled, as if her mind is lovingly replaying the memory of us together. I can't blame her, because it's the type of sensual memory that improves on the replay.

'Did I hurt you?" I ask. Her eyes are dark and haunted.

'Yes, you did," she says, shifting in her seat. "But..."

"But?"

"I think I... liked it," she says. Her eyes slide from the windshield to my face. "I loved it."

She touches her lips with her fingertips. Luna is not coy. Luna is blunt, and I like that about her.

'Good," I say, reaching across the seat to take her hand and squeeze it. I didn't know this about her, but I'm glad I'm finding it out now.

The lower level of Club Toxic is an honest-to-goodness, bona fide, BDSM dungeon. I've put this part of my life to the side for the past eighty years. I do not fancy the idea of feasting on human pain, which is why I do not drink blood straight from the source. Changelings feast on pain. My job is to vanquish them. It would not look right if I preyed on the beings I'm supposed to be protecting.

But maybe feasting on pain is okay... if she wants it too.

"I can smell the sweetness of your cunt," I say, sliding my free hand over Luna's thigh. She opens her legs to grant me access, and her scent intensifies. "I know you're turned on. Will your pussy taste as good as your blood?"

"Is that a rhetorical question?" she asks, looking at me sideways. She uses the pad of her thumb to wipe at a bit of blood caked at the edge of her mouth.

"Your blood is even sweeter than I imagined," I tell her, not bothering to answer her question. "Hot and sweet, like everything else about you."

We come to another red light. I tighten my hand on her thigh, and lean in to whisper in her ear.

"How does it feel to be under my control?" I ask.

"Scary," she says, her eyes big and round, her voice a whisper. "I'm excited. Curious. It makes me wonder what else you might do to me."

I wonder what else I might do to her, too. The implements at Club Toxic seem like too much. Or rather, not necessary.

We arrive a few minutes later, and enter the club from the rear entrance, my hand at the base of Luna's spine, guiding her through the darkened corridors and down the stairs to the part of the club reserved for the nest. Lucius Frangelico sits on his throne, as he did when I first brought Luna here, almost as if he never left. He always seems to be there, like a permanent fixture. His watchful eyes flicker over the two of us, and I give him a curt nod of acknowledgment.

Once we are in my private room, I lock the door, stroll deliberately over to the velvet couch, and sit on it. Luna stands close to the door, suddenly looking nervous and uncertain. Like she's not sure what to expect anymore, and she realizes her mouth has written checks that she's not sure she can cash.

"Come here," I say, crooking a finger at her. She looks around the room as if I might be talking to someone else, then takes a tentative step forward. I continue to beckon, and she continues to inch forward cautiously. When she's close enough, I grab her by the wrist and pull her onto my lap in such a way that she is straddling me. She trembles nervously in my arms, and I stroke her back to calm her. Her feminine scent intensifies with her desire.

She's turned on by the way I'm talking to her. The way I'm commanding her.

"You feel good sitting on my lap," I tell her.

She cuts her gaze away from mine, and her cheeks flush.

I tip her face up to me. "Don't look away from me," I say. "In fact..." I give her thigh a slap and motion for her to get up. "Get up so I can look at you," I say.

Luna smirks at me and climbs off my lap. She wore all black for our zoo excursion, and she looks sexy and badass.

"Take off your clothes," I say. My voice sounds distant and gruff to my own ears. She looks surprised for a moment, but recovers quickly and reaches for the hem of her t-shirt. She pulls her t-shirt over her head, then drops it on the sofa next to me. She's wearing a shocking pink bra of some satiny material that beautifully sets off the rich brown of her skin.

She just stands there, looking at me, with a smirk still curling her lips.

"Keep going," I say. "Take off your leggings."

She bends to unlace her boots and toe them off, then she peels off her leggings. She's wearing a thong that matches her bra.

"Finish stripping," I say. I spread my legs to give myself a little more room in my trousers, which have become tighter and more uncomfortable with each item of clothing she removes.

Luna reaches around and unhooks her bra, then tosses it onto the growing pile of black clothing on the couch. The heavy globes of her breasts spring free, her dark nipples tightened to points. Then she starts sliding her thong down over her hips, and when she's holding the tiny scrap of fabric in one hand, I hold my palm up to stop her from dropping it.

"Come here," I say. "Give those panties to me."

She inches toward me, holding out the pink material. I take them, and hold them to my nose.

Luna is neatly trimmed, her mound covered with a light furring of hair shaped like a triangle. Her pussy lips are shaved bare and swollen, and the combination is just what I prefer. I do not like completely shaved pussies, preferring enough hair to make me remember I'm fucking a grown woman.

"Beautiful, just like everything else about you," I say.

Luna looks embarrassed, and blushes under the beautiful bronze cast of her skin.

"Kneel here," I say, opening my legs further. "Open my trousers, and take me in your hands."

16

Luna

OPEN MY TROUSERS, *and take me in your hands.*

I confess, I don't know what I expected when Hermod brought me back here tonight, and the implements we're surrounded by here continue to give me pause.

Is Hermod into that *Fifty Shades of Grey* stuff? Is he going to put me on that cross thingie? Does he want to fold me over one of those benches and whoop my ass? And... do I want him to?

He pulls me out of my internal speculations when he repeats himself.

"Kneel and open my trousers," he says. His green eyes glow with banked passion. I have never been with a man like this, being bossed around like this, and I'm both excited and nervous. After a moment's hesitation, I go to my knees and look up at him, then reach for his crotch. I unbutton and unzip his jeans, and see that he's wearing boxer briefs, which are stretched over a *rather* large package. Somehow, the sight of his underwear seems ridiculous. I feel like he should have more exotic underwear, not plain navy blue briefs. Or maybe, he should be commando. His cock is large and presses urgently against the fabric of his underwear, and I'm more than a little alarmed at the idea of fitting it inside either my mouth or my pussy.

"Take me out," he says, interrupting my thoughts. I jump and look into his eyes again. They are focused, but hold a touch of amusement. His lips are curved slightly at the corners.

I tug his pants down his hips and legs until they form a puddle at his ankles. Then I slide my hands up his tree-trunk thighs until my fingers touch the waistband of his briefs. I hook my thumbs into the waistband and drag his briefs down his thighs. His cock pops out and slaps against his groin, and when I have his briefs completely off, I take a moment to admire the view. Hermod has a trail of dark blond hair down to his cock, which is huge and beautiful, just like the rest of him.

The tip is mushroom-shaped, and there is a bead of his natural lubrication there. Blue veins travel the impressive length of his shaft, and all I can do is stare and lick my lips. I want nothing more than to take the beautiful tip of his dick in my mouth. I want to taste the pre-cum gathering there, swirl my tongue over it, and suck him into my mouth until I gag on him.

"Look at me," he says. I blink and look him in the eyes. "Tell me what you want."

I don't hesitate a second before answering him. "I want to taste you," I say, my words coming out in a rush. " I want to take you into my mouth until your dick hits the back of my throat and I choke on you. I want to inhale your scent as you fill my mouth with your dick. You have the most beautiful cock I've ever seen."

I should be embarrassed at such an admission. I've been throwing myself at him whenever I get a chance, and this is not a thing good girls do. But I'm not ashamed, because this is the hottest I've ever been for a man in my life. I am desperate for him, and I'll do whatever I need to to taste him.

"Show me," he says. "Show me what you want to do."

I reach for him, but he puts a hand up.

"Show me without touching me," he says.

I'm confused about what he wants. How can I show him if I can't touch him?

"Open that slutty little mouth of yours and show me." His lips quirk with amusement again.

He wants me to make a fool of myself, by pretending to suck him off? I cast my eyes down again, not sure I can make myself so vulnerable as to mime sucking his dick while he watches me with that trademark smirk of his. I shake my head.

"I can't do that," I say.

"Yes, you can," he says. "If you want this," he gestures at his groin and his big, beautiful dick, "then you're going to have to show me how you're going to take care of it."

I weigh my options. Crouch at his feet with my tongue hanging out, pretending to suck him off like a fool? Get up and leave?

"Stop thinking," Hermod chides me. "Do what comes naturally, sweet."

I ponder this a moment, then close my eyes and open my mouth. I imagine how Hermod will taste on my tongue, what he'll feel like filling my mouth. I imagine licking along the ridge of his beautiful dick, tasting his salty pre-cum, and let out an involuntary moan of longing. The cool air of the private room chills me, raising goosebumps on my skin.

My hands, which had been flattened against my thighs, slide toward my pussy, almost without me thinking about it. I'm dripping wet, and the full-blast air conditioning brushes the wetness like a caress. But I need real friction. I need stimulation, because this teasing is frankly annoying.

Hermod must see what I'm doing, because his deep voice booms, "Don't touch yourself."

My eyes pop open and I glare at him in uncompromised annoyance. Here I am, naked and cold, acting out a pantomime of me blowing him, only to be told I'm not allowed to get myself off? He's an asshole, and I am frustrated enough to tell him so.

"I don't want you to get off yet," he says.

I sigh impatiently. "And why not?" I demand, aware that I sound like a petulant child.

He looks at me. The subtle amusement I detected earlier is now a full-blown, shit-eating grin.

"Because I said so," he says. "And if you want to do this with me, you'll need to play by my rules."

I give him another glare.

"Is that your mad face?" he asks with a tut.

I start to get to my feet, ready to walk away from this situation but, quick as a flash, I'm on my hands and knees, facing the plush purple carpeting. Hermod's hands push down on my shoulders.

"Stay where you are," he says, his voice soft and low. And close to my ear! It must be one of his funky vampire tricks. "You're beautiful. I want to keep looking at you."

I let out an aggrieved sigh, and will myself to hold still, waiting for whatever might come next.

"Turn around," he says. "Let me see your beautiful ass."

This is awkward, but I manage to stay in my crouched position while I turn around, still face down, and turn my ass for his inspection. If I thought making love to a phantom dick was awkward, this is even more embarrassing.

"Turn your ass up so I can see you better," he says. "I want to see how wet you are."

I do as he says, turning my backside to him so that he can see my glistening folds.

Behind me, I can hear him making noises as he gets to his feet. I hear him step out of his jeans and presumably leave them on the floor, then kick them away, and I'm vaguely surprised that a man who refers to his jeans as *trousers* wouldn't pick his clothing up to fold and place neatly on the couch next to him.

"You are beautiful," he says. "Truly magnificent. Your skin is such a beautiful, rich brown color, and your body is firm, yet still womanly."

His words make me feel oddly pleased with myself, but I'm not sure how to respond.

"Thank you, er, Hermod," I say.

Out of the corner of my eye, I see he's getting on his knees. His shaft is still engorged, bobbing stiffly in front of him, the head an angry, purplish color, and I am desperate to taste him.

He places a hand on my back, then runs the fingers of his other hand through my wetness. I flinch at the contact.

"Hold still," he says sternly. The admonishment is followed by a hard slap to my right ass cheek. I muffle a cry, and gasp. My breathing is shallow and ragged. I try to maintain my composure, try to hold still, but when his fingers slide over my wet pussy, my hips twitch and I push against his hand.

"Please," I gasp, shameless. "Please..."

"Please, what?" he asks. His tone is once again stern. Irritated.

"Touch me, please," I beg. "I feel like I could come just from your touch."

He chuckles. "That's not how this works," he says. "Ever since I met you, you've been mouthy. Pushing my boundaries. But if you want me to fuck you, that's not how we're going to do it. You don't boss me. I boss you."

Okay, when he puts it that way, I don't think I mind as much as I thought I would. I'm already doing things I didn't think I would with any man. I'm teetering on the brink of an explosive release, and I'm going to be really pissed if I can't get there. But Hermod turns me on like no other man.

"I understand," I say. My voice is choked with desire. Dark with emotion. I'm so caught up in this experience that standing up and walking away from him no longer seems like an option.

"I *am* going to touch you," he says. "But you're not going to come until I tell you to."

I say nothing to this.

"Tell me you understand," he demands, his voice coming in a hiss.

Coming on command is something that only happens in romance novels. I doubt Hermod can make me do it, so I have nothing to say.

"Say it!" he demands again, giving my ass a hard pinch. As crazy as it sounds, I'm looking forward to seeing his bruises on my flesh later.

"I understand!" I scream.

"Good girl!" he exclaims, then slaps my ass again, the other cheek this time. His fingers go to my pathetically swollen pussy lips and he slides a finger inside. I manage not to flinch at the mind-boggling contact, which threatens to bring tears to my eyes.

I chew my bottom lip to avoid giving voice to my desires.

"How does that feel, sweet?" He has breached the entrance of my pussy, his broad fingers probing me slowly.

"G-good," I say.

"It feels good to me, too," he says. My head is slightly turned so that I can catch his movements out of the corner of my eye, but I can't see everything. "Close your eyes, sweet. Show me with your body what you want."

So that's what I do. I stop trying to think through this moment and focus only on the sensations filling my body. His fingers have found my G-spot, and he's stroking me to a slowly building release. I let the ebbing waves of pleasure take over me until I am trembling like a leaf, my release is so close. The stroking in my pussy is matched by the pressure of Hermod's hand on my back, holding me in place as he mutters filthy words into the semi-darkness.

He tells me how beautiful my round ass is, how sweet I look shaking and crying before him, how he wants to bite me all over and make me his. All the while, I'm building, building, building—until he surprises me by stroking me inside in a move that ignites my release in a brilliant flash of white hot passion, and ordering me to climax.

"Ahhhh!" I come with a scream that feels like my lungs are emptying every last ounce of breath I have.

"Good girl," he praises. He continues to stroke me through my aftershocks, and coax me back to earth with murmured words of praise.

Afterwards, I'm reduced to a puddle of goo. I'm still in my crouched position, but my bones are gelatinous and my joints are loose. My pussy still twitches with aftershocks, and I'm trying to muster the energy to seek out his dick to give him satisfaction. I know he must be crazed with unfulfilled desire.

Hermod withdraws his fingers and leaves me, but I can't yet register the world around me enough to react. The next thing I know, I feel the displacement of air, hear the thud of pillows hitting the carpeted rug next to me, and then my hips are propped up. Hermod is back with me, his tongue licking one ass cheek lovingly. My body stirs at the stimulation, and I make a tentative move to go up on my elbows.

That's when I feel it—the sharp sting of his bite. The motherfucker is biting my ass cheek and although I should be mad about it, I'm stunned to find my pussy hops to attention at the sinful contact.

Hermod Oluffson is biting the fuck out of my ass, and I love it.

I know I'm supposed to be quiet and docile, but I lose my mind.

"Fuck! Fuck!" I scream. My pussy is drenched, and pulsing with anticipation. Almost as if he's obeying my "fuck" command, Hermod grips my hips hard, and enters me with an endlessly long thrust.

His balls slam against my clit, which twitches in pleasurable waves of a mini orgasm. Goosebumps travel over my skin and my mouth drops open at the sensation of being overwhelmingly full. I can't move because the feelings are so all-encompassing. I just hold still to allow my body to adjust to his girth and length.

Hermod is having none of that. His hips start to move in a fast, urgent pace. His fingernails dig into my flesh as he pushes into me again and again. It hurts and it feels good all at the same time, and he's not waiting for me to get used to him.

He's grunting, rutting into me like the beast he is, and he's cursing in a guttural language I do not understand. I remember the simple village that came to me in the vision I had of his past life, the first time I touched him. I remember the brute force he exhibited with each of his kills. I imagine the centuries of pent-up rage and brutality he must have endured, and suddenly, I want nothing more than to be the vessel of his blood lust and frustration.

I speak out of turn. "Bite me again!" I plead. "Please!"

One of his huge hands creeps around my neck as he bends me back in a fluid motion. I can't believe my spine is able to handle the maneuver, but while I feel pushed to a breaking point, I don't go past it, and I feel his fangs puncture the muscle of my shoulder.

Pain and pleasure mix, and I come, screaming and crying my release. I'm shaking and trembling in rapture for what seems like ages, and I'm soon joined by Hermod. He stiffens and I feel him pump rivers of cum into me as he climaxes with a roar, and another string of Old Danish curses.

This time, when I come down from my orgasm, we're floating back to earth together, and I'm safe and secure in his arms.

17

Hermod

"DID YOU LEAVE A MARK?" Luna asks, shifting in my arms. We are stretched out in the king-sized bed in my private suite at Club Toxic. The bed is covered in pure white linens, a striking contrast to her beautiful, smooth brown skin— and the bruises and fang marks I left all over her body, the result of all the spanking and biting I've done over the last several hours.

"I promised I would, didn't I, sweet?" I say, sliding my hand down to cup her haunches. Her ass cheeks are a rosy, hot pink, and at the center of one is my bite mark. She flinches when I grab her there, which causes my dick, which had gone soft due to exhaustion, to perk up and take notice. It goes from limp to steel pipe in a matter of seconds, and is pressed against Luna's thigh.

She gives me a cranky look, and scoots her hips away from me. She cocks an eyebrow at me. "Seriously?" she asks. "Dude, I need a break. When do you plan on sleeping?"

"I see you still aren't clear on who's in charge here," I

growl, giving her opposite ass cheek a hard slap. "I'm not sure I want a woman who can't be enthralled."

She narrows her eyes at me and gives me a saucy reply. "What, you don't want to work for it?"

I smile in spite of myself. The truth is, I don't think I'd know what to do with a woman I can glamour into doing whatever I want her to. What would be the fun in that? But, I decide to keep giving her shit.

"Well, there's work," I say, cocking an eyebrow at her, "and then there's high maintenance. You, sweet, are high maintenance."

It's the middle of the night, and I'm still too buzzed on sexual adrenaline to crawl into my crypt and rest. I'm certain this has not happened to me in years, if ever. Luna has changed me.

And she doesn't like my latest assessment of her, as evidenced by her continuing to move away from me on the bed. I do not let her go. I entwine my legs with hers, pinning her down. She makes token movements to evade my grasp, but I stop her. It's been on my mind that she needs to stay with me—for a variety of reasons, principal among them being that hunting changelings is easier with her around. I'm not sure how this is happening, but I want to know more. I can't help but think her abilities were heightened as a result of being mugged.

"What happened the night you were attacked?" I ask. Her face registers surprise, then wariness at my question.

"I was walking home late that night," she says. "I usually got a ride from a co-worker, but I had to work late, and told her that I'd get an Uber. When I left work, the bus that goes right in front of my apartment was already there, so I decided to save a few bucks and take that. The last thing I remember is getting off the bus. I woke up in the hospital days later."

"Did you ever find out what happened?"

"The police told me later," she says. "There is a video of the whole thing from the ATM across the street from my apartment building. I've never seen it, but apparently there was enough evidence for the police to find the guy. He's in jail, awaiting trial."

"Will you have to testify?" I ask.

"I don't want to," she says with a sigh. "I don't know what I can add to the trial. I don't remember any of it."

I make a mental note to talk to Slash about this. Surely the skinny little hacker can find out the details of her case, including the name of the guy who assaulted her, where he is being held, etc. "I'm surprised you can go out at night these days," I tell her. "Considering what you went through."

Luna casts her eyes downward, her fingertip drawing circles on the hairs on my chest.

"When I first got out of the hospital, I wouldn't go out of my apartment at all," she says. "When I tried to go out during the day, the sun, the noise, and all the people... it was too much. Weird, yeah, but I only feel safe at night."

I pull her closer to me, running my tongue along her neck. She shivers. Her skin is so hot against my mouth, and it's as if the blood coursing in her veins is screaming for me to taste it.

"You should watch the tapes," I say. "It will help you remember. You won't have to be afraid anymore."

She pulls away from me, her eyes large, dark and haunted. She frowns. "No," she whispers, shaking her head.

"Yes," I say. "Maybe not today, but soon. You need to watch the tapes, and testify about what that man has done to you, even if you don't remember what happened."

"No," she repeats. "I don't remember, and I don't want to. And that part of my life is over. I don't want to go back to that day."

When she tries to disengage from me, I don't let her. She struggles against me.

"Soon," I say. "You need to confront what happened to you so that you can move on."

"Let me go," she says. She looks angry with me.

"It doesn't work that way," I tell her. "You opened a can of worms when you let me taste you. I'm not inclined to let you go."

Her frown deepens, and she tries to pull away from me again.

"You need to see this through," I tell her. "You told me yourself. You said I scared you. Excited you. I think it's mixed up with the experience of being attacked. You're not over that, despite what you say."

"That's sick," she declares, her voice husky with emotion. Her eyes brim with tears, and I wipe them away with my thumbs when they spill over.

"We won't talk about this anymore tonight," I tell her. "But we will talk about it. Someday. In the meantime…"

"In the meantime?" she asks, her bottom lip trembling.

"In the meantime, we are done with ravishment for the evening. We need to rest."

She studies me with pursed lips. "Okay," she says, rolling over so that her back faces my front. I pull the blankets over us, and wait until I hear her breathing deepen. But her body is still tense.

"What's the matter?" I ask.

"Why is there a dungeon here?" she asks.

"When I give you pain, it makes your blood much more sweet to the taste," I tell her. "Club members bring their… guests to the club for this purpose."

"Is that why you call me *Sweet*?"

I reach around her and cup her full breasts, pulling her tighter into my body. "There's much more to you than your blood," I tell her. "You are a brave woman to take on what-ever dangers you might face when you go out at night. You didn't think twice about coming with Slash and me to put down changelings. You are fierce and strong, and yes, sweet, but I thought that before I even tasted you."

She's quiet for long moments, obviously taking in this information. She runs a hand up my forearm. "Do you use the dungeon?"

"No," I say. "We have a sort of... blood bank... for the club members."

"You use the blood bank? You don't usually drink from humans?" She turns over and faces me in the dark. The lights are dim, and she's searching my face for answers.

"I haven't for a long time," I tell her. "I hunt creatures that feast on human misery. I don't want to *cause* misery."

She purses her lips thoughtfully. "Then, what are you doing here with me?"

"You sort of forced my hand—" I start to say, but she puts a finger on my lips to make me stop talking.

"Forget I asked," she says. "I can see you falling into a mind fucking spiral. I think you don't trust your feelings when it comes to me. I make you feel something you don't want to feel."

I blink at her, not sure what to say. Part of me wants to ignore what she's just said, even though I know there's a kernel of truth in it.

"Sleep," I say, realizing the instant the words come from my mouth that I can't just command her to sleep. "I will hold you until you go to sleep, then I must sleep in the crypt. When you wake up, I won't be in bed with you."

"Wouldn't want to get too close," she says, her tone chiding.

Before I can say anything else, she turns her back to me again. "Goodnight, Hermod."

"Goodnight, sweet."

18

Luna

I'M AWAKE WELL before Hermod the next morning, but he's no longer in bed with me. Sometime during the night, he must have gotten into the crypt off to one side of the huge private room we are locked in. He told me he would do so when he held me as I fell asleep last night. This morning, his side of the bed is cold.

I sigh, staring at the ceiling. I'm not sure what time it is, but it must be pretty early, since I seem to be constitutionally unable of sleeping past 8 a.m. If I were a sensible person, I would simply relax and enjoy the crisp white sheets, the luxurious minky blankets caressing my skin. As I stretch, I feel the aches and pains from the possessive, dominating fucking Hermod put on me the night before, and want to see how I look. I get up to relieve myself, realizing there are no mirrors anywhere. Not in the private room, and not in the adjoining bathroom.

I make a mental note to ask Hermod whether the legends are true, that vampires do not cast reflections. The lack of mirrors might just be the product of the vampires' lack of vanity. Given how good looking all of Hermod's nest-mates are, perhaps they don't need the constant self-affirmation. If they are all as old as Hermod, chances are, they already know how they look.

Since I don't have a reflective surface in which to examine myself, I look at my naked body as best I can. My breasts are swollen, the skin ruddy from being roughly manhandled the night before. There aren't many marks on my torso, but when I turn sideways to look at my butt, I see a series of dark bruises and two pinprick fang marks on my ass. I touch the marks on my skin, relishing the soreness.

I didn't think I'd enjoy being roughed up like that, but as I think back on the carnal memories, I find myself getting excited all over again. My pussy dampens, and an involuntary smile curves my lips. My eyes slide over to the crypt in the corner, which is a plain black box with a metallic surface.

Not wanting to wake Hermod when he might actually need the rest, after I've freshened up in the bath, I dress in the previous night's black outfit, strap on my fanny pack, and venture out into the club.

All is silent in the club. Apparently, the rest of the nest also likes to sleep late. I sit at the bar, feeling a bit like a kid on Saturday morning, when the parents are sleeping in and I'm left to my own devices. Only, there is no cable TV to entertain myself. Also, I'm hungry.

I sit and drum my fingers on the bar, wondering what to do with myself. I realize I haven't checked my email in hours, and my clients will soon be sending me research requests. I really should track down a computer.

As I sit there, wondering what to do with myself, Evangeline appears from behind the bar, startling me.

"Oh, hi there," I say, blinking in surprise.

The little blonde woman is the picture of efficiency as she produces a menu and sets it in front of me.

I take it, shooting her an incredulous look. "Do you ever sleep?" I ask, opening the menu.

She gives me a rueful smile. "Not so much these days," she says.

Does that mean she's a vamp too? Would it be rude to become out and ask her?

As I ponder this etiquette question, Evangeline speaks up.

"Where's your man?" she asks, a slight smile curving her lips.

"Still asleep, apparently," I say while perusing the menu. It's mostly normal fare, what one might expect to find at a diner. "No O-Neg on the menu?"

She chuckles. "That's the upstairs menu you're holding," she says.

When I squint in confusion, she clarifies. "It's what the vanillas eat." I guess I don't look like I understand, so she raises her eyebrows and looks for signs of comprehension. "The humans?"

It takes me a moment to get it.

"Oh, so you have human visitors?" I ask. "And they eat upstairs?"

"Yeah," she says.

I order a burger and fries, and hand the menu back to her. "What time is it?"

She consults her watch. "About 12:30."

I frown. "As in, after noon?"

"Yes, afternoon." She chuckles again. "Most of the nest won't be up again until sundown. This is still pretty new to you, isn't it?"

"Do you mean the vampires, or the BDSM?" I wave a hand to make my point. "Yeah, this is all pretty new to me."

"It takes some getting used to." She's keeping herself busy by wiping down the bar. "Are you settling in okay?"

"Um… I don't think I'm settling in at all," I say, wondering what Hermod has been telling his nest mates. "I'm just hanging out for a couple of weeks. I actually have a life and everything."

She looks surprised. "Really? You two seem pretty compatible," she says. "You know, comfortable with each other. I thought you two were a couple, not like any of the other girls he's brought here."

Other girls? But didn't Hermod say he doesn't bring other women here?

"You've seen him bring other women here?" I ask slowly. If I'm not misunderstanding her, then Hermod lied to me last night when he said he doesn't bring women to the club. Of course, I don't care if he has other women for a little harmless, mutual fun, but what's the point in lying about it?

"Slash mentioned it to me," she says with a nonchalant shrug.

My confusion must show on my face, because her eyes bug for a moment. Then she frowns.

"I think I must have said the wrong thing," she says, putting her hands up in a *don't shoot the messenger* gesture. "Forget I opened my mouth."

As I sit there, brooding, she steps away briefly to retrieve my lunch order. Suddenly, I'm ready to get back home to my own life. It's later in the day than I thought, and I haven't been to my apartment in weeks.

When Evangeline returns, I ask for a to go bag for my meal.

"Since Hermod apparently needs a few more hours of beauty rest, I'm going to take my burger and fries to go, okay?" I say.

A frown creases her pretty face. Evangeline reminds me

of one of the sister wives from that cable TV show, *Big Love*. She looks like the younger wife with the long, blonde hair and babe-in-the-woods, innocent eyes.

"You sure about that?" she asks. "You don't need a ride or anything, do you?"

I'm not waiting around for Hermod, who has shown he's not as trustworthy as I thought. I barely know the guy and while I'm annoyed and even a little hurt that he felt he needed to lie to me about his past relationships, it's none of my business, and I'm not worried about disease or anything like that. But his pet name for me, the vulnerability I thought he was showing me... all of that was a lie. I have a life of my own, and I don't need to deal with this man's bullshit.

I helped him with his hunt and, presumably, the threat to me has been eliminated. I'll go back to my apartment, eat my lunch, and get back to my own life.

"I'll leave Hermod a note," I say. "Do you have a pen and paper I can use?"

I dash off a quick note for Hermod, which I leave with Evangeline. I leave Club Toxic ten minutes later, setting off for a bus stop that will get me to my apartment in no more than an hour or so.

When I let myself into my apartment, all the warm, fuzzy feelings I woke up with have long evaporated. I'm second-guessing the night before.

The sex just wasn't as good as I remember it being, I tell myself as I sort through the piles of junk mail that have accumulated in the past couple of weeks.

My life was in peril last night, which had my adrenaline pumping madly in my veins. Hermod and I had been cooped up in his house for two weeks before the confrontation with the changelings, with sexual tension crackling between us the entire time. The fear, combined with the lust we've had for each other from the beginning, pretty much guaranteed that by the time we got around to actually having sex, it would be memorable.

Hermod clearly knows his way around a woman's vagina, and knows how to initiate a BDSM novice like me into taking pleasure from pain. Before last night, I hadn't had sex in months, so it stands to reason that all these factors put together would result in a paradigm-shifting sexual experience.

I clean my apartment vigorously as I tell myself that I can easily replicate the experience with any other similarly inclined sexual partner. There must be tons of guys out there who want to spank a woman on the ass while fucking and biting her. True, the number of men who will do me with an Arnold Schwarzenegger accent, then cuddle me afterwards, is probably vanishingly small, but who said life is perfect?

Somehow, being back in my apartment re-grounds me in my regular life. Club Toxic, Hermod, and changeling chasing were diversions. It's time for me to put my sexual awakening aside and get back to my humdrum life.

I dig out my old netbook and check my email for any new forensic genetic genealogy assignments, but find I don't have any. While these are the most interesting assignments, the bread and butter of my work is skip tracing research. In a sense, what I do isn't too different than what Hermod does, except I don't do apprehensions. I find people who aren't where they are supposed to be through unconventional means, and let the bail bondsmen do all the running around.

I don't have any requests for skip tracing either, which is a bummer. I haven't been doing the same kinds of phone networking I usually do in the past couple of weeks, since I've been distracted by Hermod.

Since I'm self-employed, I make a habit of paying my rent a few months in advance, as a hedge against homelessness. Even if I don't have new work for months at a time, I don't have to worry about how to support myself. Occasionally, I pick up a few shifts at an insurance call center in town. The last time I did that was when I was mugged.

Even though I always make sure I have a financial cushion, whenever I am not inundated with requests for my services, I experience moderate to severe panic. For example, in the absence of any pending assignments, I feel compelled to visit my online bank accounts to reassure myself that I'm not going to have to find a cardboard box to sleep in. I know this won't really happen. If worse comes to worst, I can move back to El Paso and live in my childhood bedroom in my parents' house.

When I pull up my bank account, expecting to find a few thousand bucks in financial security sitting there, I'm stunned to see the actual balance is about ten times that.

"What the hell?" I whisper into the quiet of my apartment. I last checked my account two days ago. Sometime between now and then, someone has deposited a million dollars in my checking account.

For a few minutes, all I can do is look at the screen, unblinking, just... looking at it.

I sit there for so long that eventually a session timeout message pops up. This is what eventually makes me blink. I run my finger over my trackpad to continue the session, scrolling down to my account history to see how this happened. I see only a cryptic ACH notation from the night before—a deposit of $1 million USD. This, of course, answers none of the many questions I have about my change in financial circumstances.

Once the information begins to sink in, my first thought is: *I'm rich!*

My second thought is: *Hermod.*

Or, more accurately: *Slash.*

Hermod and Slash are behind this. There can be no other explanation.

I am not sure how to process this, so I continue to stare blankly at the glowing computer screen as evening gathers outside my window, casting shadows across the rooms of my lonely little apartment.

Then there's a knock at my door, and even before I look through the peephole, I know who is there.

I open the door to Hermod Olufson, who is leaning against the door frame with a shit-eating grin on his handsome face.

19

Hermod

"Hello, Hermod," Luna says. She's wearing faded jeans and a V-neck red t-shirt. Her feet are bare and her face, makeup-free. Her dark brown gaze is intense to the point of hostility, and she has an eyebrow cocked in challenge.

"Hello, Luna," I say, watching her intently for clues as to her mood.

When I awoke at sundown, I was surprised to find her nowhere to be found at Club Toxic. She'd left a note for me with Evangeline, stating she'd enjoyed her time with me, but that she needed to get back to her "regularly scheduled life".

After I had a short conversation with Slash, asking him to make a deposit to Luna's bank account and dig up information regarding her assault earlier this year, I'd cleaned up and gone looking for her. Part of me knew she wouldn't go through the trouble of trying to hide from me, so I found her in the first place I looked: her apartment.

From what I can see of the place, the entire apartment unit could fit in the master bath of the timeshare where I'm currently staying. In the short time I've known her, Luna doesn't seem in the least interested in my obvious wealth and resources.

"I had expected to see you when I woke up this evening," I say.

"Why did you expect that?" she asks bluntly. "We didn't make any plans beyond last night, did we?"

She has her hand on the door as if she's one step away from slamming it in my face.

"I thought we... hit it off," I say, wondering if I'm using the American idiom correctly. It doesn't come close to capturing just how exciting the sex was with her last night.

"We hung out," she says. "We had sex. It was great sex, then it was time for me to leave."

I frown at her. We had sex, but it was mind-blowing. The most exciting encounter I've had with a human in many, many years. But sex was just one part of what made the encounter so explosive.

"Why did you leave me this note?" I ask, taking it from my back pocket and holding it out for her to see. "It wasn't very nice of you."

"Nice?" She sneers, crossing her arms over her chest. The motion pushes her breasts up, and I'm momentarily distracted by the sight of her plump globes pressed together to form an attractive cleavage. "It didn't have to be nice. We both got what we wanted. Now it's time to move on."

"I don't want to move on," I say. I'm aware of the fact that I sound like a petulant child, but Luna isn't making any sense. Why does she want to move on from me? Didn't she enjoy the time we've spent together?

"Really? Well, I do," she says. "I live in the real world where things like jobs are necessary. Sitting around, waiting for some guy to wake up doesn't appeal to me. By the way, you can tell Slash to reverse the deposit into my bank account. I don't need your money. Good night, Hermod."

She goes to close the door in my face, but I put my hand up.

"Wait. Aren't you at least going to invite me in?"

Luna pokes her head over the threshold and glances up and down the corridor in front of her apartment door.

"I'm not inviting you in, because I don't want you just showing up whenever you feel like it," she says, lowering her voice so that it's barely audible. "That legend is true, isn't it? You can't come in unless I invite you, can you?"

"Well, yes—" I start to say, but find I'm talking to the reinforced steel of her apartment door. The woman has slammed it in my face, and she's done it so quickly that she might as well have blurred to do it. I stand there, blinking, then let out a frustrated sigh, wishing that I had the power to enthrall this woman. I hear the deadbolt turn, and the security chain rattle on the other side of the door.

"Luna, I have your things with me," I say. Don't you want your computer and phone back?"

"Leave them on the doorstep, and go," she says.

If I were a religious man, I'd be praying for patience right about now. This woman is impossible.

"This isn't a safe neighborhood," I say. "I'm not going to leave your things out here where they can be stolen."

I hear her sigh on the other side of the door, then the shuffling of feet and, finally, the sound of the door being unlatched and unchained. She steps out into the hall, but now she's wearing her Doc Martens, and a fanny pack around her waist. She's shrugging into a dark blue jean jacket, and she smells like cocoa butter and some kind of fruity soap.

"Let's go," she says, glaring up at me. "Take me to your

car, give me my stuff, and tell me your business proposition."

The evening is cool enough that I can see Luna's nipples, taut with the cold, clearly outlined through the fabric of her bra and t-shirt. Her demeanor is brisk and impatient, and while on the face of it, she is complying with me, it's clear she doesn't want anything to do with me.

"Just like that?" I ask, puzzled. "I expected more resistance from you." With Luna, I'm finding I do not know what to expect from her from one moment to the next.

"Clearly, leaving you a polite note isn't enough to dissuade you," she says, eyes flashing with irritation.

"Why do you want to dissuade me?" I ask, still confused as hell by this woman.

"If I kept arguing with you, you'd never go away," she gripes. "So, we'll go to your car, you can give me my things back, and give me your business pitch. I'll then pretend to consider your proposition before I shoot you down. Okay?"

I get into the driver's side and close the door, then turn to wait for Luna to get in the car. She parks herself in the passenger seat, but leaves the door on her side open, her foot on the running board, evidently poised to get away from me.

I look at her, tilting my head to one side to study her.

"Why are you so eager to get away from me?" I ask.

She gives me a sidelong glance. "Why are you so eager to try to seem like someone you aren't?"

I must look as confused as I feel, because she gives me a disparaging look and rolls her eyes.

"Evangeline told me that Slash told her that you have women at Club Toxic all the time."

I have no idea what she's talking about.

"Evangeline is mistaken," I say.

Luna seems not to have heard me, and she's revved up to

rant at me. "You know, I really don't care what you did before you met me. But you didn't have to lie to me about all the other girls you've caused pain to and," and she slices the air with a disdainful wave, "sucked on."

I stare at her, dumbfounded, because there is so much to unpack here, and little of it appears to be accurate.

"I have not lied to you," I say.

"Nice," she says sarcastically. "I haff not lied to you." She repeats my words back to me, exaggerating her delivery to mimic my accent.

"I don't sound like that," I say, offended.

"You sound exactly like that," she says with a smile.

I sigh. "Close the door and we'll go somewhere more private," I say, starting the car. "I don't want to discuss this here."

It's her turn to sigh in resignation. "Fine, but if you don't bring me back, I'll be grabbing an Uber back home."

"Fine." I wonder when this annoying little human will get over the notion that she's in any position to call the shots in this relationship. I'm an 1100-year-old vampire with supernatural abilities. She's a thirty-year-old human whose superpowers seem to include a mild psychic intuition, as well as an uncanny ability to irritate me with her sarcastic mouth. She's no match for me.

As I drive, I realize I'm not sure where I'm going. We're in a working class part of town, near what appears to be an elementary school, a baseball field, and a gymnasium. I pull over in a parking lot in front of the baseball field and turn off the car, turning to find Luna studying me with wide, frightened eyes.

"Do you feel that?" she asks. Her breathing is shallow.

"Feel what?"

"There's something here that's triggering my fear

instinct," she says. "I take it you haven't noticed it? Why did you pull over?"

I shake my head. "No, I haven't. I just felt compelled to pull over here. Like at the truck stop."

Luna's face is strained with trepidation, her eyebrows drawn together. "I think there's something dangerous here," she says. "You brought us here, so I assumed you felt it too. You didn't?"

"No," I tell her, keeping my voice at a whisper. "You did this. You brought us here."

Her eyebrows go up in surprise and she shakes her head, as if denying my words would make them any less true. "I can't do that."

"This is what I wanted to discuss with you," I tell her. I open my mouth to say more, but my attention is diverted by motion in the playground outside the elementary school. Luna sees it as well.

"What's that—" she starts to ask, but I place my fingers to her lips, to stifle her.

"Wait here," I say.

I get out of the car, close the door quietly behind me, and head for the playground. And despite the fact that I very clearly told Luna to stay in the car, I hear her do the same. I turn around to give her a stern, chastising look, but she squares her shoulders and lifts her chin, as a teenager might do in a show of defiance. The defiance I will be punishing later.

For now, I give her an exaggerated eyeroll. I blur to the playground.

There's a changeling, completely shifted to its insectoid form, perched on a dome-shaped monkey bars structure. Underneath, there's a little brown girl cowered into a fetal position, her legs tucked tightly against her body. She can't be more than nine or ten years old, and her curly dark hair is tangled, and matted with wood chips and dirt. Her brown eyes are wide and vacant, and she's shivering with the night time desert chill. She's wearing a yellow smiley face t-shirt and pink leggings covered in illustrated sugar skulls. Her feet are bare.

"Hey, asshole," I say, trying to catch the creature's attention. Since changelings have poor hearing, and I can blur almost noiselessly, the changeling didn't hear me approach. It whips around quickly to confront me, its long, muscular tail grasping the monkey bars for balance.

"Hunter," it hisses at me. It cranes its neck and lets out a high-pitched shriek.

"That's right, here to kill you, as I did your other nest mates," I say casually, striding towards the creature until the tips of my boots are no more than a few feet away from the edge of the monkey bars. The little girl blinks her big brown eyes at me, and trembles. The creature puffs up its body, assuming an attacking stance.

"After I kill you, I'll just have two more of you fuckers to put down," I say.

The changeling breaks off a section of the monkey bars with its tail, and suddenly, I'm on my back with the green scaled creature pinning me to the soft playground mulch with one of its claw-like hands. Above me, its eye color swirls—the usual mixture of sulfuric yellow and green—as it focuses on my face. It holds out a free hand to take the metallic section of the monkey bars, and I realize in a flash what it intends to do. It's going to use the broken-off piece of playground equipment as a stake.

In a panic, I struggle to free myself, but I'm completely pinned down and the creature is amazingly strong, despite it being so wiry. I thrash and attempt to flip myself over to escape, but I have an *oh, shit* moment when I realize I have nothing to hold onto to gain any sort of leverage, and panic begins to settle over me.

"You will die, hunter," says the changeling. Even with me completely at its mercy, the stupid creature can't resist monologuing like some damned supervillain.

But too bad for the changeling, it is not to be.

I hear the distant rumbling of a muscle car engine, which puzzles me, until I realize what's happening.

Headlights flash across the changeling's face mere seconds before the GTO smashes into it. Before I have a chance to register what's happening, the undercarriage of the car passes over my face, the fabric of my t-shirt tears, and when I go up on my elbows to see what the hell is going on, I see red tail lights as the GTO comes to a stop.

The changeling must have been caught in the undercarriage of my car, and it is stunned. The long, scaly tail twitches ineffectually as it weaves and struggles to its feet.

The driver's door opens and Luna quickly jumps out. She takes in the heap of creature misery near what's left of the back bumper of the car, then glares at me.

"Well, don't just lie there," she screams. "Get the fuck up!"

20

Luna

WE PARK DOWN the street from a nearby fire station.

"I'll walk her to the station," Hermod says. "You stay here. If there are surveillance cameras, they won't see me, but they will see you and the car."

"Vampire hoodoo?" I ask, realizing that the question I had upon awakening this morning—whether or not vampires cast reflections—has been answered with Hermod's bossy instructions.

"Something like that." He grins. "I mean it, too. Stay here." He emphasizes his point with a poke to my chest.

"Fine," I sigh.

Hermod gets out of the car, helps the shell-shocked little girl out of the backseat, then gathers her in his arms. As I watch, he strides down the sidewalk with her cradled close to his chest. A few feet from the front door of the station, he sets her on her feet and stands there looking down at her. I can't make out her features from this distance, but Hermod is reacting to the look on her face by going down on his haunches and opening his arms. She throws herself into his embrace and hugs him tightly.

Okay, so he's not a complete asshole, I tell myself sternly, not wanting to give in to the heart-melting sensations assailing me at the sight of him holding the little girl he has just rescued. Hermod Olufson may be good at hunting changelings, but that does not mean I can trust him.

I have no obligation to this man, no matter how many urchins he saves from the clutches of supernatural evildoers. We are going to continue with the evening's discussion, I'm going to say "no" to whatever he wants me to do, and I'll go on my merry way.

He gets back in the car and starts the engine, then turns to me, his expression uncharacteristically low key and thoughtful. "Thanks for the help," he says.

I squint at him. "Help?"

He steers the car away from the curb, and doesn't speak again until we come to a stoplight. "It was touch and go for a while there," he says. "I appreciate your crazed driving skills, although I've never had the experience of being run over by a car before. That was new."

"Let's just go get this conversation over with, okay?" I roll my eyes at him.

"All in due time," he says. "By the way, I wish I could have seen the look on your face when you ran that changeling over. You must have looked like a Valkyrie going into battle."

I smile in spite of myself, because yeah, despite the terror I felt in that moment, I quite enjoyed running down the creature. That shit was fun. I'm pretty revved up after that fight. Sexually revved up.

Out of the corner of my eye, I look Hermod up and down. His t-shirt is ripped in places, and his hair is mussed, but he looks none the worse for wear considering he's someone who has recently tussled with, then vanquished, a giant praying mantis-type creature. He looks good enough to eat, actually. Or, at least, good enough to nibble on.

Soon, we're pulling up to his swank house in his posh neighborhood. There's another car parked in front of the house, a little dark compact car that has *Slash* written all over it—figuratively, not literally, though my blood-sucking buddy is nowhere to be seen.

"Are you expecting company?" I ask.

"Slash is already inside," Hermod says grudgingly. "I asked him to meet us here."

"What do you have against Slash?"

"He's hot for you," Hermod says bluntly. "I don't share well."

I frown at him because, frankly, I don't see why he'd be jealous of Slash.

"I'm not a plaything," I say, my feminist hackles raised. "You don't own me."

He had been looking out the windshield, and he turns his head slowly to look at me. He lets out a snort of laughter, then grabs the back of my neck with his large hand, and hauls my face to his for a bruising kiss. My body arches into his before I even realize I'm doing it. My lips part under the assault of his kiss, and he sucks my tongue into his mouth.

"Mmmph..." I say, more than a little ashamed of the way I make a fool of myself whenever I'm in his arms. My body tingles all over from his possessive kiss, my breath is shallow, and I melt against his hard body.

He breaks the kiss, and speaks in a whisper against my lips. "You belong to me," he says. "Say it."

I shake my head vehemently, because I will do no such thing. This man has nothing to offer me other than a place in line to be his living, breathing feedbag. Well, nothing except the money he put in my bank account.

"Belong to you?" I say. "I don't even like you."

But it's a lie, because I'm just a hair's breadth away from straddling this man's thighs and impaling myself on him; I want him so badly.

He places a hand between my jean clad thighs.

"You're a liar," he says simply. "You want me to bite you all over. You want me to fuck you until you scream. The sooner you admit it, the sooner I'll give you what you need."

I scoff. "You don't have anything I need."

"Is that right?" he asks.

"Yes—" I start to say, but the next thing I know, his tongue invades my mouth. He's kissing me breathless, his large hands around my throat, pressing hard enough to leave a bruise later. I can say nothing more in this moment. I can only feel him sucking on my tongue, choking off my air supply until tears prick my eyes and my pussy screams with the pent-up need for release.

He's sucking my tongue in earnest now, and I'm teetering and dizzy from the heightened sensations, until I feel his fang prick the meaty flesh of my tongue.

"Ahhhhh!" I scream as my entire body explodes with the breathtaking explosion of pain and pleasure. My mouth fills with the metallic taste of my own blood, and he smashes his lips into mine. My body trembles with the aftershocks of my brain-fogging orgasm.

"You will admit it," he grunts into my mouth. His lips and tongue are slick with my blood, my panties are wet with a release that came upon me so suddenly, I am dizzy and reeling with sensations.

"Never," I insist, frowning and shaking my head.

He chuckles. "You are fun to play with." He tilts my chin up and stares into my eyes. "You resist, but you will come to my way of thinking, and your surrender will be sweet."

He reaches into the glove box and extracts a white cloth

handkerchief, which he uses to carefully wipe away the blood on my lips. The deep red is a startling contrast to the pure white of the fabric, and I find myself staring at it.

What does it say about me that I enjoy it when this man inflicts pain on me? Why do I love being bitten by him? These are questions I thought I'd left behind when I left Hermod's bed earlier today and frankly, they are questions I don't want to think about. I don't think I like this part of myself.

My shoulders sag as I study the white cloth and as these thoughts ricochet through my mind.

"What are you thinking," Hermod asks, startling me out of my reverie.

When I meet his eyes, I see interest and teasing in the blue depths of his gaze.

"Nothing," I say, attempting to disengage from his hold on me. "Why is Slash here?"

He chuckles again. "Slash is helping me with a project. We'll get a briefing and once he's gone, you and I will talk. We have much to discuss."

"Okay," I say, avoiding his eyes.

I follow Hermod inside, through the spacious foyer and into the grand dining room, which is set up like a conference room. Slash is sitting at the head of the dining room table, which is ridiculously throne-like, tapping away at the laptop in front of him.

The hacker's eyebrows go up until they almost touch his hairline, and he grins wickedly at me, an expression that causes Hermod to scowl in distaste. Slash makes a wiping gesture to the side of his mouth.

"You have something on your mouth," Slash tells me. I thumb the area, and discover what feels like dried blood on the corner of my lips. Hermod must have seen it, but didn't mention it to me, the bastard. Marking his territory, like a dog pissing a circle around me.

I sigh and excuse myself to freshen up in the luxurious powder room near the front door. When I return, Slash is still seated and Hermod is standing directly behind him, leaning over his shoulder to get a look at the screen. Both their faces are illuminated by the laptop screen, which casts a bluish glow across their features.

"What are you looking at?" I ask, not sure I actually want to know.

The two men exchange looks.

"Get up," Hermod says to Slash, who complies. Hermod waves me over and gestures to the seat Slash has just vacated. When I sit, I see the screen is completely black. It's completely innocuous, but I feel a prickle of unease anyway.

What is this all about?

Slash reaches around me and wiggles the mouse. There's a still shot of a video screen, and it takes me a moment to figure out what I'm looking at.

"Is that—" I start to ask, because it looks like me, there on the screen. It's a paused surveillance video, grainy and poor quality, but I recognize my legs, my Doc Martens, and the messenger bag I used to use before I was mugged.

"Slash, can you give us a minute?" Hermod asks.

Slash leaves the room, closing the dining room door behind him.

Hermod pulls up a chair beside me. "Start the video," he says, nodding at the paused image.

I blink at him, disbelieving, because he and I have already discussed this. "I told you I don't want to look at this," I remind him.

"And I told you, start the video," he says.

I cross my arms over my chest. "No," I say. I try to push

myself away from the table, but he stops me by putting a hand on my thigh.

"Never mind, I'll do it," he says.

"I don't want to—" I begin, but he reaches around me and moves the cursor to the play button arrow. The video starts, and my stomach drops.

On screen, I'm stepping off the city bus and waiting for it to pull away before I cross the street. My messenger bag bumps against my hip as I adjust the shoulder strap. I pause, presumably waiting for the stoplight to change. My head turns to one side as I watch the bus go hissing down the block.

In the outer edge of the frame, on screen, I see a tall, muscular figure wearing a jean jacket and a baseball cap approach me from my left.

As I watch, I ball my hands in my lap, twisting my fingers with anxiety. My heartrate speeds up. I don't want to keep watching, but now I'm finding it difficult to look away. I roll my lips inward, and press them together.

"It will be okay," Hermod says from his place at my side. He places a hand over mine, and squeezes.

I was so engrossed in the action on screen that Hermod's deep voice surprises me, and I jump. With my hand over my heart, I gasp and stare at him.

"How did you get this?" I ask. The footage must have been locked away somewhere, not easily available to just anyone. Hermod gives me a pointed look, then glances at the door Slash has just exited through.

"Slash," I say.

Hermod starts the video again, and I turn my attention back to the screen.

Video me turns toward the sound of approaching footsteps. As I watch in growing horror, the shadowy figure grabs my messenger bag. I hold onto it almost reflexively, as the man tries to yank it away from me. On the screen, I stubbornly hold on to my bag as my attacker continues to wrest it away from me.

In the struggle, my attacker's hat pops off and I see a shock of shaggy, pale hair. His face, which had been hidden from the camera's view, is revealed in profile.

Hermod freezes the screen with a click of the mouse.

"John Wayne Bluett," he says. "Thirty-two years old, heroin addict, has a rap sheet as long as your arm."

It's odd to hear the colloquialism come out in Hermod's guttural accent.

I give him a questioning look, then sigh. "Slash," I say.

"You need to confront this, sweet, and I will help you," he says.

I'm blinking back tears. "I was so stupid," I say on a choked sob. "I should have just taken an Uber, instead of trying to save a few bucks. If I hadn't been out that night—"

"He would have found someone else to hurt," Hermod says.

I think about everything I lost after the attack. The ability to go out during the day without fear. When was the last time I was able to go to the grocery store, or to the movies, or even to go out with friends? The sense of safety I used to take for granted is gone forever. All because of one stupid, stupid decision.

He starts the video playing again. On screen, I struggle against my attacker. There is no sound, but I can imagine how I must sound as I struggle to stay on my feet, my arms lashing out ineffectually, my legs flailing. Finally, the struggle ends when John Wayne Bluett picks me up with his drugged-out strength, and slams me to the ground. On screen, I continue to struggle, but he's intent on subduing me, and I watch in horror as he slams my head to the ground repeatedly. My face is turned up and, at the time, I must have been looking straight into his eyes, but I have no memory of any of it.

My struggles gradually cease. My hands loosen and fall away from the strap of the bag. A shadow slowly grows and spreads around my head. I can tell it's blood.

In the video, my blood is soaking my hair and staining the pavement underneath my head. I let out an involuntary shudder. The man in the video looks around furtively, stupidly allowing himself to be caught on camera.

"I only had fifty-three dollars and change," I find myself saying. "He let himself get videotaped. It was so stupid, so pointless."

I can't hold back my sobs any longer. I burst into tears, turning away from the monitor, hot emotion bubbling and chewing at my chest. Hermod stops the video replay, picks me up, and holds me in his arms.

I sob against him, burying my face in the firmness of his chest, and his arms slide around me and hold me close.

"Shhh," he says, stroking my back gently.

"Why didn't I just let him have the bag?" I sob.

"Because it's not how you're made," he says in a low, soothing voice. "You're a fighter."

I let out a watery laugh. "Or maybe I'm just stupid."

"No, you're not," he croons. "You ran down a changeling with my car. Do you know how many people don't even know how to drive a manual transmission? You are a badass."

I laugh again through my tears, aware that I'm blubbering all over this man's t-shirt.

"As strong as you are, you need to let this go," he says. "You need to let go of your guilt, and you need to stop blaming yourself for someone else's actions. You have a right to walk in your own neighborhood without being attacked."

"Maybe you're right," I say. I realize it's time to compose myself. I put a hand on his chest and push away from him to look into his eyes.

"I know I'm right," he says. He's holding onto me, not letting me go when I attempt to get away. He has an odd look in his eyes, one I can't quite place.

I frown at him.

"That's why I brought you here tonight," he says. "To talk about how you're going to get over blaming yourself, and how you're going to let this pain go."

21

Hermod

STILL SEATED at the dining room table and with Luna cradled to me, I call out to Slash, instructing him to take his laptop and go. Luna keeps her face tucked into my chest the whole time, her body soft against me.

By the time I take her up the stairs to my master bedroom, the tension has leached out of her body and she is limp in my arms. I take her into the bathroom, undress her, and run her a bath. The stress of discovering the little girl at the playground, killing the changeling, and forcing Luna to confront her past have taken a toll on my sweet, and fear rolls off her in waves.

But the night isn't over yet, because in order to be free of her past, Luna must forgive herself for something that wasn't her fault in the first place. It's time for her to stop living in fear.

I lower her into warm bath, and when she sighs, I feel a sense of pride that I can bring her this kind of relief. She's drowsy, her eyes droopy and half lidded, as she sinks into the water.

"You are a strong woman, sweet," I say. "The strongest woman I have ever met."

"I'm not," she murmurs. "Not really. I couldn't let that thing stake you without doing something about it. I'm guessing that staking thing is real, right? If it drove that monkey bar piece into your heart, you'd be dead right now?"

"Yes, it's true," I say. I squeeze a dollop of cocoa butter soap on a sponge and begin to bathe her. I run the sponge over her shoulders, her arms, her breasts, and torso. She doesn't resist.

"You would have done the same for me, if the situation had been reversed," she says matter-of-factly.

"I would have," I agree. "But that's not what I meant, and I think you know that."

She says nothing in response. Her dark eyes, which had been watching me curiously, drop to contemplate the bubbles floating on top of the water.

"Tonight, you are going to purge your guilt over what happened to you," I tell her. "And I'm going to give you an opportunity to give your life a deeper purpose. Then, I'm going to punish you."

Luna's eyes clear of their drowsy haze instantly and she sits up in the tub, causing water to slosh onto the marble floor.

"Careful," I admonish. "When you get water on the floor, it makes it slippery, and I don't want you breaking your neck getting out of the bath."

She scowls at me, eyes narrowed to slits. "Punish me for what?"

Her face is angry, but I can hear her heart beat with anticipation at my words. The pulse at her throat jumps and her breathing shallows. The idea of me punishing her has her excited.

"Punish you for allowing yourself to be mugged," I say easily.

"But you just told me I need to stop blaming myself for what happened to me," she protests, looking confused.

I kneel in front of the tub, squeeze more soap onto the sponge, and tap her knees with my other hand. She takes the hint and lets her legs fall apart so that I can cleanse the space between her legs.

I rub the sponge in circles over her womanhood, watching her carefully for her reaction. Her mouth is set in a stubborn line, almost as if she's daring me to make her feel better.

"You were the reason we wound up at the playground," I say. "The two of us together tracked the changeling, and killed it. Your trauma is a gift, one you shouldn't squander out of misplaced guilt."

"You gave me the money to bribe me, didn't you?" she says petulantly.

"I gave you the money because you deserve to be free of the past. And because you earned it. Believe me, if all I had to do was spend a few bucks to locate changelings, I'd spend ten times more than I did."

"A few bucks?" she asks, her eyes wide and incredulous. "A million dollars isn't *a few bucks*!"

I finish washing her, get to my feet, and hold my hand out for her to take. She rises from the water like a mermaid I'm extracting from the ocean. I envelop her in a fluffy white robe and pick her up in my arms again.

My bed is an elaborate four-poster canopy made of mesquite wood. The duvet is white and fluffy, and the canopy is draped with gauzy white netting.

I place her in the center of the bed, where she pulls the robe tightly around herself. She looks lost and vulnerable perched on the white coverlet.

I join her on the bed, peel off the robe, and toss it to the floor. I'm a little surprised she doesn't resist. She just keeps looking at me with her big, curious brown eyes.

I lean in for a kiss, taking her delicious mouth with mine roughly until her lips fall open with a moan and she lets me plunder her mouth. I push her back on the bed, spread her out so I can see more of her, and kiss her roughly. Her body is soft and she squirms under my touch. My body comes alive from the contact, my dick instantly hard and throbbing for release. When we break the kiss, she's breathless.

"This isn't how this evening is supposed to go," she pants. "Instead, you're trying to seduce me."

"Sweet, there is no trying involved," I tell her. "I am seducing you."

"You know what I mean." She scowls.

"Are you complaining?" I ask, eyeing the pulse jumping in her neck. I want to bite her there, taste her blood filling my mouth, lick every last drop as it pulses out of her body. I bend my head, and nuzzle her.

"I-I'm just saying..." She gasps.

"What are you saying?" I murmur against her neck.

"This isn't going to work," she says. "Your glamour doesn't work on me. You can't charm me with your vampire mind games."

I trail a hand down her body to settle at her womanhood. It is warm, swollen, and wet. I stroke her with my fingers, delighting in the way she squirms underneath my touch.

"I don't need mind games," I point out, realizing with mild shock that my words are true. I don't need to enthrall Luna to bend her to my will. "You are as wet as you've ever been before, aren't you? Tell me, where should I bite you tonight?"

Her eyes go wide at my words, but she says nothing. Her

feminine scent is intense, and teases my nostrils and hardens my cock.

I capture her wrists in my hands and straddle her body, my legs on either side of her hips. I raise her hands over her head in a blur as she blinks in confusion. With her arms awkwardly positioned, I snap the shackles I'd earlier attached to the headboard by a chain, around her wrists.

I take an obscene amount of pleasure in her changing expressions as the confusion in her eyes turns to shock, then anger.

"What the hell?" she yells, pulling against the restraints. She wriggles and bucks beneath me, trying to get me off her, apparently forgetting that I'm both bigger and stronger than she is.

"I told you, I don't need to charm you," I say.

"So you just... restrain me?" she shouts, pulling hard against the cuffs.

"Exactly," I say, as she shoots daggers at me with those mysterious, dark eyes of hers.

I go back on my haunches to study her. Because of the way I have her cuffed, she cannot flip herself over to evade my penetrating gaze. Luna is completely naked, and her magnificent body is mine to do with as I please. Her curvy little body is on full display, from her soft, round breasts, whose dark nipples are taut with arousal, down her flat belly, to the apex of her thighs.

"Open your legs," I say. I tap the inside of one knee to illustrate what I want her to do.

Unsurprisingly, Luna does not comply. All I get in response is a glare.

"Stubborn woman," I mutter, and get off the bed. I stride over to an armoire in one corner of the room and open the doors. I hear rustling on the bed behind me, and a quick glance over my shoulder confirms Luna is craning her neck to see what the hell I'm doing. She tugs at her wrist restraints again, then winces at the discomfort.

"Be careful," I say in a chiding voice. "Those cuffs aren't fur-lined. I'd hate to see your wrists get chafed."

"Uncuff me!" she demands, as if she's calling the shots. It's been so long since I've been with a woman like this that I've forgotten how much fun it can be.

"No," I state simply, and turn back to my cabinet of toys. I mentally debate the choice of implements at my disposal, finally settling on restraints that hook under the bed and will keep her thighs wide apart, so that I can get a good look at her pussy. I also hold a ball gag in the other hand. I hold both items up so she can see what I have.

She's breathing hard—panting, really—but I can't tell whether she's even more angry, or even more turned on. She narrows her eyes at me. "What the hell are *those*?"

"You'll see," I tell her.

She opens her mouth to protest, but I blur to where she is. I am able to gag her and tie her knees open before she can register what is going on. Her eyes widen in genuine surprise and true horror at her predicament.

I loom over her once more, this time between the toned brown thighs I have propped open with my restraints, and look down at her. It's on the tip of my tongue to say something like, "Cat got your tongue?" but not even I am that cruel. She's breathing hard around the gag, and saliva pools in the corners of her mouth.

"Now, you're going to listen to me," I say, looking deep into her dark, bottomless eyes. "You are not responsible for what happened to you. You did not get John Wayne Bluett addicted to drugs. You did not make him attack you at the bus stop. You need to let it go."

She rolls her eyes at me, and gives me an aggrieved look.

"The best way to get over it is to quit your job and help

me kill changelings," I say. My logic is undeniable. How can she possibly object?

"Mmmph! Mmmph!" she says behind the ball gag.

I sigh. "You're going to need more convincing, aren't you?"

Luna narrows her eyes at me again. She looks *pissed*.

"Luckily, I'm up to the task," I say. I scoot down the bed and park myself between her thighs. The scent of her womanhood is heady. Sweet and a little musky, and strangely, a lot like cherries.

I bend my head, and give her a long, rough lick, from her taint to her clit.

She hisses and keens against the gag, and her back arches off the mattress.

Her taste explodes on my tongue, her scent fills my nostrils, and I dig in to feast on the prettiest, most delicious pussy ever created. She writhes and thrashes as much as her restraints allow, and I eat her like she's a ripe peach. I drag the flat of my tongue over her clit, pressing down hard, enjoying the way the tiny nub hardens under my tongue.

I can feel she's close to climax, but I don't want her to yet. I ease the pressure, enough to let her catch her breath and back down from the orgasm. I sit back on my haunches again, waiting for her breathing to slow down and, gradually, her eyes lose some of the glazed expression she'd had.

"Convinced yet?" I ask. I trail the flat of my palm over her inner thigh, enjoying the view of her pussy with its neat strip of short hair. Luna's eyes are no longer unfocused. They are smoldering hot. Determined.

I watch intently while she shifts on the bed, makes direct eye contact, and nods.

22

Luna

I'M WEAK. So weak.

Because Hermod is so good at sexing me up, I'm completely weak and at his mercy when he makes love to me. He knows exactly how to touch me, exactly how far to push me to get me right to the edge of climax.

I have never been restrained during sex before, and if Hermod had asked me beforehand if I would let him, I might not have said yes. But, I'm finding I enjoy the sensation of being helpless and vulnerable to him. I'm not afraid to place my trust in him, and while I was initially leery of being tied up, under his skillful touch, I'm now teetering on the edge of orgasm.

When he asks me if I'm convinced I should work with him, all of a sudden, the answer is easy.

"Convinced yet?" he asks.

I find myself nodding quietly, telling him non-verbally that I'm ready to embark on a new phase in my life. Seeing myself being attacked on screen was difficult, but Hermod was right to make me do it. I realize now that I'd given the attack too much room in my mind and heart, I'd let it cast too long a shadow in my life. My quirky brand of agoraphobia has had me afraid of human connections, afraid of the daylight, and I realize that I've been hiding under the guise of protecting myself.

I realize now that I have to testify at the trial, and now, I'm not so afraid to do it. I mean, I don't *really* want to re-live the attack, but I can't let John Wayne Bluett get away with attacking me—not to mention the other people he must have hurt over the years.

As soon as I nod my head, I feel a weight I didn't realize I'd been carrying lift from my shoulders and my soul.

Hermod returns my nod with a smile. He looms over me again, and reaches behind me to unfasten the ball gag. As I move my jaw to loosen the stiffness, he trails his large hands down my body, placing the flats of his palms on my inner thighs. My legs are still wide open, leaving me spread-eagle and utterly exposed to his lusty gaze.

"We're going to have so much fun together," he says.

He bends his head and runs his tongue up my thigh. My body responds almost all on its own, bucking against the restraints, surging to meet the surprisingly rough texture of his wet tongue. It occurs to me that he's tasting the skin right over my femoral artery.

"Do you want to... bite me there?" I ask, suddenly curious about how powerful his desire to taste my blood is.

His eyes close slowly and he grunts. "It's too dangerous," he says. "The arteries there are as big around as your finger. I would gorge on you, but you would die almost instantly."

"Have you ever done that before?" I ask, intensely curious about his answer. My voice is dry and husky.

"Yes, when I was... new," he says. His face clouds with tension, and I wonder what happened to him so many years ago, before banked blood became readily available. He rolls away from me and retrieves a small bottle of water, which he holds to my lips. I take a long drink, relishing the feel of the cool water sliding down my throat.

"My hunger was blinding back then," he goes on. "My thirst was insatiable."

His voice is more guttural than I have ever heard it before, and his face is clouded with emotion. I wonder what it must have been like for him. I wonder how he would react if I told him about the vision I saw the first time I touched him. Would he be angry?

For a moment, I simply watch the play of emotions across his face as he replaces the bottle of water on the bedside table. When his eyes meet mine again, I see sadness in them.

"I... think I saw your home, that first time we touched," I say. "I know you told me a little bit about it before, but I had visions the first time we touched. I'm sorry, I should have told you before, but we weren't exactly buddies back then, were we?"

His eyes spark with interest at my revelation. "What did you see?" he asks in that soft, accented voice of his. I'm completely vulnerable now, completely open and exposed... and safe with him. Will he also feel safe enough with me to let me share the pain he experienced centuries ago?

"They attacked your village," I say. My brows knit together as I remember what I saw in that vision weeks ago. My words come out in the same confusing rush I felt when I first experienced the frightening vision. "It was a vampire horde, wasn't it? Very tall men, attacking your village in the middle of the night. Color flashed across the sky. It was the northern lights, wasn't it?"

He says nothing at all and, for long moments, we just stare at one another.

"The changelings... they were disguised as us, and they

were taking over the part of Denmark where my village was," he says. "My mate... my wife... we were the last survivors. The nest of vampires tracking the changelings found us and tried to save us. In the end, I was the only survivor."

His words hang in the air between us. Nothing I say can take away the pain he must be feeling now.

"Why did you stay with them?" I ask. "The vampire nest?"

"I was looking for revenge," he admits. "I was powerless when the changeling horde arrived. I needed to do something to stop them."

"Is that why you want me?" I ask.

"Yes... no..." He runs a hand through his hair and furrows his brow. "It is, but it's not the only reason."

Hermod looks frustrated, almost as if he's trying to find the right way to explain this to me. His motives may seem mercenary, but aren't I attracted to him because I feel safe with him? Because I know that when I'm with him, I know nothing bad is likely to happen to me? How is that not just a bit mercenary on my part? Hermod is at least being honest with me.

"I don't care," I say suddenly. "It doesn't matter. Please finish making love to me. I'm so revved up that if I don't come soon, I think my head will explode."

He flashes me one of his rare, toothy grins, and reaches for my thigh, giving it a squeeze.

"I can make something else in you explode," he says.

I roll my eyes and quirk my lips. He hovers over me, skimming the flats of his palms over my thighs. His hands are rough and calloused. Goosebumps prick my skin from the light abrasions, and I shiver.

"Have you done this before?" he asks suddenly.

"Done what?" I ask.

"Let someone tie you up, then fuck you."

I sigh. "No, but you've introduced me to all sorts of new things. Praying mantis critters who turn into people, and attack. Vampires. I think BDSM is really pretty minor in the scheme of things, don't you think?"

"Brash until the end, aren't you?" he asks, quirking an eyebrow. "Whatever will I do with you?"

"Fuck me, I hope," I say, I raise my eyebrow at him.

Hermod stands next to the bed, removing his clothing slowly as I watch. He removes his torn t-shirt, kicks off his heavy boots, then shucks off his black jeans. He's gone commando today, and the sight of his nude, muscular body being slowly revealed as he undresses never gets old.

His erection is large and proud, veined and upwardly jutting, curved towards the muscular planes of his belly. The bed dips when he places a knee on the bed and crawls up to me. He hovers over me, that smile of his curving the edges of his lips and lighting his cool blue eyes. Up this close, they are a remarkably pale blue, like faded denim.

Our gazes lock and hold as he positions himself between my legs. When my eyes drift down to where our bodies are about to be joined, he takes my chin between his thumb and forefinger, and tips my face up so that I cannot look away.

"Look at me," he says. "I want to see your eyes when I enter you."

He begins to slide into me slowly, filling me inch by inch, as he looks deep into my eyes. The sensation of being wide open to him, of his considerable girth stretching me, takes my breath away.

"Your pussy is so tight," he grunts.

"What does it feel like?" I ask.

"Like a snug, wet fist," he hisses, biting out each word every time he pushes into me. My body slides up the bed with each punishing movement of his hips. His face still holds a trace of the pain of memory, a grimace of cruel passion as he barrels into me.

"What does it feel like to you?" he asks.

"Like you're holding back on me," I say. "You're not going to hurt me. At least, not like this."

His eyes, which had been intent on mine, travel over my body, taking in every restrained limb in turn.

"You are too bold for your own good," he reminds me. "One of these days, this little quirk of yours is going to get you into trouble."

I give him a meaningful look, because what he's saying isn't exactly news to me.

"You're helpless," he goes on. "You cannot move. You can only take what I give you. As little or as much as I give you."

He keeps up a measured pace, burrowing his thick cock deep inside me. My pussy trembles around his cock, practically grasping at his engorged, hot flesh, because the steady pace is annoying. It's not enough to get me off, but too much to ignore. In my mind's eye, I see his cock curving up inside me, the helmeted head battering my G-spot, but it's not enough to make me come.

My breath hitches with every thrust and retreat.

"I need to finish," I pant, growing more desperate for release by the moment.

"Tell me, sweet," he implores me. I can tell he's trying to keep his pace steady, as before, but his hips stutter and he gives me a sharp jab, so hard and so pleasurable that my eyes roll back in my head and my pussy spasms.

It's not enough, though. It's still not enough, and somehow, I know what I need to do.

I need to let go of my pride.

I need to let go of my fear.

I need to let go of everything that I *thought* made me safe, and embrace what actually *does* make me safe.

"Please, I belong to you," I say, realizing that I've never spoken truer words. "Please make me come."

It's a subtle shift, a small adjustment in the angle of Hermod's penetration, that finally sends me over the edge. My body arches and strains as I explode all around him with a high-pitched scream that erupts in waves of vibration from deep in my chest.

"Sweet!" is Hermod's cry when his release comes upon him in great pulsing waves. I feel his dick twitching as he pumps streams of cum into my quivering pussy.

He collapses on top of me, pressing me into the duvet, his large body covering mine as he collects himself.

When I shift subtly beneath him, he rolls off me abruptly and, in a blur, he removes my restraints and massages my wrists and knees. I'm as weak as a newborn kitten in his arms, utterly spent and completely safe. He pulls back the duvet and places me on the bed, then joins me. He pulls me into his arms and cradles me close to him, his front to my back, then covers us both with the heavy duvet.

I feel calm and pleasantly weary, ready for sleep. It occurs to me then that Hermod probably isn't ready for rest, and won't be for hours. He's just holding me long enough for me to fall asleep.

"Will you be here when I wake up?" I ask.

"No, I'll be in my crypt," he says. "I'll have Slash send someone here at dawn to help you gather your things and bring them back here. A human who can tolerate the sunshine. When you return, we will make a plan to track and kill the remaining changelings in the clutch."

I think of the prospect of going out in the daylight tomorrow to retrieve my things, and I tense up.

"Will you be okay, going out in the day?" he asks.

"I... think so," I say. "I did it when I left you at Club

Toxic. Of course, I was spitting mad when I did that, and my anger was stronger than my fear in that case."

"You really should have simply asked me whether I'd brought other women back to the club before you jumped to conclusions."

"I suppose you're right," I say drowsily. "And you'll still be asleep when I get back, won't you? It's going to be interesting, having a relationship with someone whose schedule is the opposite of mine."

"You can adjust your schedule, can't you?"

"Eventually," I say.

"Eventually?"

We chuckle together.

"Great minds think alike," he says.

"I think it's a combination of my abilities, and your vampire hoodoo at work," I counter. "How much more creepy will this get, I wonder?"

Hermod holds me, and strokes my body as I drift off to sleep.

23

Hermod

I KNOW the moment I emerge from my crypt that Luna isn't in the house. She should have been back from her mission to retrieve her belongings hours ago, but I do not sense her presence.

My security cameras confirm the GTO is still parked in the circular driveway. The cameras also catch the fading light of sundown as it streaks over the desert. I tell myself she must have been held up somehow as she collected her things. While her apartment seemed small and sparsely furnished when I visited her the day before, it's possible she has more belongings than I realized. If she doesn't show up by nightfall, I'll simply go out, track her down, and bring her back.

As soon as twilight has faded into night, I'm at the front door of the timeshare mansion, preparing to do just that. I open the door, keys in hand, and find none other than Slash standing there.

I let out an aggrieved sigh, annoyed by the sight of him.

"What are you doing here?" I demand. Slash brushes

past me and enters the house, his laptop tucked under his arm. He heads for the dining room, the room we've been using as a makeshift conference room, and places the laptop on the table.

I blink in disbelief, then follow him.

"I don't recall inviting you in," I say, annoyed by his presumption.

Slash cocks an eyebrow at me. "You already invited me in, days ago," he states. "Surely, you know you only need to invite me once, for one of our kind to consider it a blanket invitation?"

I open my mouth to light into him, then decide it isn't worth the trouble. "What are you doing here?" I demand. "I don't have time to play games with you. Luna is missing—"

He puts a hand up to silence me. "I know all about that," he says, his eyes focused on the screen and his fingers tapping away at the keyboard. "I sent the servant to help her, remember? Would you like to know where she is?"

Finally, the man has something useful to add to the proceedings.

"You know where she is?" I ask. I round the table to stand behind him and view his screen. There's a still frame of a video there, similar to the image he managed to download from the Tucson Police Department evidence database, which showed the footage of Luna's attack of months ago.

This time, the footage is of the courtyard of Luna's apartment complex. I open my mouth to ask what, exactly, we're looking at, but Slash speaks before my lips can form the words.

"I took the liberty of installing cameras around Luna's apartment complex," he says with a theatrical raise of his eyebrow. "When the club minion didn't return to report back to me at sundown, I suspected foul play."

I find myself grateful that Slash took the liberty of

spying on my sweet, and annoyed by the unnecessarily dramatic presentation of the information he's found. I wish this fool would simply get to the point, and again open my mouth to tell him so, but he puts up a hand and gives me a little wave of acknowledgement.

"You're welcome," he says. "I thought you might find this footage of interest."

I run a hand through my hair and count to ten in my mind. Slash starts the video, which shows Luna walking up to her apartment door, key in hand, with a smile on her lips. Beside her, there's a tall woman with long, dark hair. The taller woman is wearing jeans and a dark pea coat against the chill of the desert evening. Luna chats animatedly with the other woman, although the video either has no sound, or the sound is muted.

"Who's that?" I ask.

"Her name is Leann," Slash says. "She hangs out at Club Toxic."

"Is she—" I start to ask. The woman is somewhat familiar to me.

"She's one of the sweetbloods," he says. "I might have sipped from her a time or two."

I nod in understanding. I don't partake in sweetbloods, and haven't had blood that wasn't from a bank in decades. Because of this, I don't take much notice of the women used as feed bags in the club, except in passing.

As we watch, the women enter the apartment. Slash fast forwards through the footage, making the two figures on screen hasten about their business with jerky motions. As we watch, the women go back and forth with boxes and suitcases, disappearing off camera, presumably to take Luna's belongings to the car. They prop the door open with what looks like a small brick, presumably to facilitate a more efficient moving process.

At one point, as Luna and Leann leave the screen again, a shadow appears to one side of the frame. It's a man wearing a baseball cap. He slips into the apartment quickly, letting the door bump closed against the brick door stop. The next thing we see is Leann entering the apartment, but she doesn't come out again. Luna soon appears and enters, then there's no activity for several long moments, until she appears with the man and they leave the apartment. In the video, Luna looks frightened and stressed. He's holding her close to him awkwardly with one arm, and has a hand pressed to her side, through his jacket. I sense he has a pistol or knife or some other kind of weapon held to her belly.

Blistering anger wells up in me at the prospect that my sweet is in danger. I must find her, bring her back, and punish the man who has her.

When his face appears on screen again, I realize who he is.

"John Wayne Bluett," I mutter, and shoot Slash a questioning look. "But how?"

"There must have been some sort of paperwork mix-up, and he was released on a technicality," he says with a shrug. "I'm still looking into it, because I can't find a record of the prisoner transfer."

"When did all this happen?" I ask, nodding at the screen.

"Around two in the afternoon," he says. "He attacked Leann and tied her up inside the apartment. Eventually, she got herself free. Her car was gone. Luna was long, long gone."

"It was pretty stupid of him to do that," I comment.

"This could be his third conviction in ten years," Slash says. "He's facing a long mandatory sentence if he's convicted. At this point, he may feel he has little to lose by taking Luna."

"Any idea where he would have taken her?" I ask.

If what Slash is saying is accurate, Luna doesn't have much time, because surely John has kidnapped her with the intention of preventing her from testifying against him.

"No idea," Slash says.

I sigh, frowning as I consider how to proceed.

"I'm going to go by her place," I say.

"Did she ever invite you in?" he asks. "What do you think you're going to be able to do if you can't even go in?"

It's a good question, because this could be a waste of time. But what else can I do? Perhaps being where she was taken will give me a clue as to where she is, and how I can find her. At the end of the day, I have nothing else to go on. This isn't like tracking changelings, where I can follow news reports of strange happenings to find my prey.

I set out for Luna's apartment, and Slash accompanies me, tapping away at his phone screen as we drive, researching known associates of the man who has taken Luna.

Standing in front of her apartment door, I feel as helpless as I ever have in all my 1100 years. I feel a faint vibration of Luna's presence here, more than I experienced when I was here before, standing on her doorstep and waiting to be invited in. But it's not enough to make sense of, or do anything about, so I'm frustrated to no end.

"What do we do now?" Slash asks as we sit in the GTO in front of Luna's apartment. It's not even midnight, and I could prowl the streets as I sometimes do when I'm looking for my prey, hoping something pings me and provides some sort of direction. I've found changelings this way, but only with Luna's influence to guide me.

It occurs to me then that perhaps I can find something of her by visiting the spaces where we shared time together.

This is how Slash and I find ourselves back at Club

Toxic, where my private room sits empty and untouched since the last time I was here.

I enter the room alone. Her essence lingers from our lovemaking, and the metallic scent of her blood hangs in the air. I'm getting a vibration similar to the one I received at Luna's apartment. It feels like a flutter in my belly, a subtle sense of unease that I can't quite put a name to. Somehow, in this room, feeling traces of Luna's energy around me, I know she's not in immediate danger. But that won't last for long, and meanwhile, I don't know where she is, nor can I protect her.

She may be okay now, but, she also isn't *here*. With me, where she belongs.

Frustrated, I leave the private room and enter the bar area.

It's the middle of the week, and not yet midnight, so the club is not at all busy. There are a few members gathered around, looking bored. It is a common characteristic of my kind. Having lived for so long, most of what happens in life ceases to hold interest for the vast majority of us, and we are left with boredom.

Evangeline is behind the bar tonight, and she gives me a speculative look, a hand on her hip as she sizes me up. We make eye contact and I stroll over to sit at the bar.

"What can I get you?" she asks.

"Nothing," I say, waving a hand dismissively. If Evangeline hadn't told Luna that I made a habit of bringing women to the club, my sweet would never have been upset, and would not have left me the day before. Luna would have trusted me earlier, would have invited me into her home, and we wouldn't be in this predicament right now.

I'm not sure what to make of this woman, but I decide it's time to learn more. I sit at the bar, and hook my heels on the barstool frame.

"Where's your girl?" Evangeline asks, leaning her elbows on the bar to stare me down.

"She's... not here," I say.

She frowns at me, and gives me another speculative look. "Is everything okay?" she asks, looking cautious, almost as if she's not sure her questions are welcome.

"No," I say. "Everything is not okay."

"You sure I can't get you something?" Her eyebrows are up and her face is inquisitive. "You take from the blood bank, don't you?"

I do normally take from the bank, but I no longer have any desire to. I want to taste Luna.

I *need* to taste Luna.

"Not tonight," I say.

"You look like you've got it bad for this girl." She chuckles.

I glower at her.

"Is *she* okay?" Evangeline asks. There is true concern in her large blue eyes.

"You told her I made a habit of bringing sweetbloods to the club," I accuse.

"Haven't I seen you with anyone here?" she asks, looking confused.

"No," I say. "You have not."

Evangeline frowns. Shrugs.

"My bad," she says dismissively. She picks up her cloth and wipes down the bar top.

I just stare at her, unblinking. Is it worth trying to explain to her the sequence of events her careless words have put in motion? Probably not.

"When are you bringing her back?" Evangeline has her back turned to me, wiping down the top-shelf liquor bottles the club keeps on hand for human guests.

"I don't know," I say. "Soon."

"Don't wait too long to bring her back," she says.

Nothing about this situation makes sense right now.

I'm an old man. Old in body. Old in years. But I feel like a child right now.

Luna makes me feel young. Not young, as in optimistic. More like young and uncertain. Wet behind the ears.

Evangeline turns back to me, and places a glass in front of me. It's a wine glass filled with human blood. I pick it up and hold it to my nose, inhaling the coppery scent. I put it down again, pushing the glass back toward her.

"No, thank you," I say. I slide off the barstool and walk away.

"Bring her back again sometime!" Evangeline calls out.

I hold up a hand and wave as I leave.

I can't be at Club Toxic right now. I need to find Luna.

24

Luna

WHEN I LEFT my apartment with John Wayne Bluett, it was with the knowledge that appearing to acquiesce to his demand that we "talk this out" was the only way to stay alive in that moment. The gun he held to my side persuaded me that going with him was the best idea, at least in that situation. Despite the fact that he had assaulted me in the past, and the fact that I'd returned to my apartment to find Leann unconscious on my kitchen floor and her—*my*—assailant standing over her, I realized that the best thing to do was to play along and wait for an opportunity to get away from him.

He didn't look agitated in the least, not like the man I saw in the video Hermod showed me. In fact, even though I saw him attack me in the video, I'm having a hard time believing he'd actually be able to do it. His demeanor is too calm, too relaxed, to suggest he'd be anything other than some fast-food worker who spends his off time playing *Super Smash Brothers* in his mother's basement. I feel confident that I can handle anything John Wayne Bluett can dish out.

Which is why I was pretty pissed when we reached Leann's car, which we had parked in the courtyard to better move my things, and the asshole attacked me before I even knew what was happening.

There's nothing like being hit over the head and stuffed in a trunk of a car to make you question your life choices.

I'm not sure how long I was out, but when I come to, I'm completely in the dark.

I'm on the floor, on something soft but dirty.

It's a mattress, I realize. Shakily, I get to my feet and wince when my head feels like its swimming, then I fall to my knees again. I rub the back of my hand against my temple, as if doing so will erase the pounding headache that makes my head feel like it's splitting in two. I inhale deeply, on my hands and knees on the mattress, trying to catch my breath. Nausea causes my stomach to pitch and roll, and I swallow against the bile threatening to rise in my throat.

Where am I?

I'm shivering. Shivering so hard that my teeth are chattering, and it's a wonder I can't hear them clacking out loud.

I lean into the wall, which is some kind of cold metal. A little rough under my fingertips. I don't know where I am, and I do not like it.

I swallow my bile. I swallow my panic. I'm shaking, and I'm realizing that all my recent choices have led me here. If I hadn't left Club Toxic in a huff, I could have spent the day being lovey-dovey with Hermod, rolling around in bed and being spanked, pinched, and fucked.

And bitten.

I would be sore and satisfied right now, instead of sore and groggy.

I explore the rough, metal walls, creeping along, using my fingertips to guide me in the pitch dark.

Where am I? Where the fuck am I?

I stumble when I come to the edge of the mattress and, like a fool, I trip over my own fucking feet. I go down again, landing on my knees and the heels of my hands. Because apparently, it's not bad enough to be kidnapped and locked in some metal box, I also have forgotten how to walk upright.

I get up again, biting my lower lip hard enough to draw blood.

An image flashes in my mind: the first time I kissed Hermod, straddling him in his car like the brazen bitch I was pretending to be, and letting his fangs graze my tongue. The taste of my own blood, the way he pulled me onto his lap and devoured my mouth so greedily when he got a taste of my blood.

Do you have any idea what you're doing?

You're like a little girl trying on her big girl panties, aren't you?

Those were his words to me, right before he kissed the shit out of me in his car, right before he took me to the club and ravished me, giving me the most satisfying sexual experience of my whole entire life.

"No, Hermod, I have no fucking idea what I'm doing!" I whisper-yell into the darkness. "And yes, I was trying on my big girl panties. It turns out they didn't quite fit."

The absurdity of my situation hits me, and as I sit back on my ass and rub my hands and knees against the pain, I start laughing. First, I'm chuckling to myself, low, so that I don't alert my captor to my conscious state.

Then I hear the sound of metal against metal, and realize that the door to this dungeon is being opened.

"Luna Reed…" hisses a ghostly voice.

I look into the darkness, in the direction of the voice, willing my eyes to focus, trying to force myself to see. But it's still dark—so dark that I can't see anything.

I recognize this voice. It sounds exactly like the creature that tried to strangle me with its tail.

"Who is that?" I scream. My voice is hoarse and ragged. I sound desperate.

I hear light, quick footsteps in the dark, rapidly approaching me, and I do not have time to react before a body slams into me and I'm on my back, my limbs pinned to the mattress.

"Scream," the changeling hisses. Its breath is damp and hot on my cheek.

"What?" I ask.

"Scream," it hisses in its awful, slithering voice. "Scream, and bring the hunter here, so we can finish him."

This doesn't make any sense. There's only one of them... isn't there?

More light footsteps echo in the space, answering my unvoiced question. I bite my lip in order to avoid giving the creatures what they want. My breath comes in fast pants. I'm pinned to the mattress, unable to push the creature off me, struggling to move.

Hermod! Hermod!

My mind screams in a panic, and I'm shocked to get an answer.

Sweet! Where are you, sweet?

Something must show in my eyes, even in the dark, because the creature speaks.

"Good," it says. "I see you've made contact."

This thing really needs a speech therapist, because it sounds super creepy when it attempts human language.

In the next moment, my limbs are no longer being pressed into the mattress. I scramble to my feet and follow the direction of the retreating footsteps, but come up against a closed door. I feel around to find a latch, but without success. Sighing, I lean against the door, shoulders sagging, and break down sobbing.

Don't come, Hermod, I say in my mind.

Somehow—perhaps it is the stress of the situation—the link I have shared with Hermod since the very beginning of our relationship has somehow expanded while also becoming more refined. When he replies, it sounds like he's whispering in my ear.

How can I stay away? he says. *You belong to me. You are mine. Mine to protect. Mine to love.*

My heart lurches and flutters like a million butterfly wings, beating in my chest.

Love. He said, *love*.

There are a bunch of them here, I say, ignoring his last words to me. I need to focus on preventing him from coming here, and walking into an ambush. *They're going to kill you.*

Not if I kill them first, is his reply.

Cocky, aren't you? I chuckle to myself.

I've been killing changelings for centuries. I've got this.

His accent transmits in my mind, which is weirding me out a bit.

The last time you went up against a changeling, I had to rescue you, I remind him.

Minor details, he says. *Sit tight, I'll be there soon.*

25

Hermod

I SAID I would be there soon, but the truth is, the psychic link I share with Luna isn't a precise thing. It's not a homing beacon, as I would expect, but more like a ping that goes on and on but provides no specific direction. It is a bit like living in a house with a smoke detector that needs a new battery, but being unable to pinpoint which one is beeping.

I wander the darkened streets of Tucson aimlessly, changing direction whenever Luna's signal gets stronger. Eventually, I find myself going into what appears to be an abandoned trailer park with a few outbuildings scattered around. Luna could be anywhere in these many acres of ramshackle buildings.

And not just her. The changelings are certain to be around here somewhere, lying in wait to attack me and take me down. Changelings always hatch from clutches of nine eggs, and by my count, there are only two left in Tucson.

I wander the trailer park deliberately, listening for any sounds that are out of the ordinary, waiting for the sense of

Luna's presence to grow stronger. I find myself at the edge of the park and headed for the outbuildings, including an old, battered Quonset hut. It's locked with a heavy metal padlock.

I creep closer to the metal building as silently as I can.

"Hermod? Is that you?"

I have grown so accustomed to hearing my sweet's voice in my head that I'm a little shocked to hear her talking out loud, and it takes me a moment to figure out where her voice is coming from.

"Luna?" I whisper. It's obvious she's in the metal hut. I put my ear to the door and grab the padlock, rattling it.

"Let me out!" she demands.

I yank the padlock and it comes off in my hand. I open the door, and Luna throws herself into my arms. I hold her tight, savoring the feel of her small body trembling against mine. Her face is streaked with tears, and anger boils in my blood.

The creatures that kidnapped my sweet will pay.

I hold Luna away from me to get a good look at her, to see whether she has been harmed. Her brown eyes are huge and round.

"Hermod, watch out!" she screams, just as I feel a weight landing on my shoulders.

A long, muscular tail wraps around my waist. Luna falls hard, and she winces when her back hits the ground. I am lifted off my feet, then slammed to the ground beside her.

Our heads turn simultaneously and we stare at each other, blinking.

"Hermod—" she says, reaching for me. Another tail slips around her waist and she is snatched away from me.

"Hermod!" She screams, reaching for me, but the changeling that has her flings her around like she's a ragdoll. When I try to regain my feet, I'm jerked away from her and suddenly, I'm looking into a pair of huge eyes, pupils dilated to pinpoints, irises swirling green and yellow.

"Hunter," it hisses. "Time to die, hunter."

I roll my eyes. "You always say that, and I always kill you," I say. I set aside the fact that one almost staked me the night before, and go for bravado. "I'm going to kill you and your friend, too."

The creature's mouth opens, exposing rows of sharp teeth that are alarmingly white against the dark circle of its maw and the green scales of its skin. A forked tongue emerges and flicks over my face.

"Are you afraid yet?" it asks in a voice that is barely recognizably human. "I've always wanted to feast on the pain and fear of one who hunts us."

The creature is squeezing me so hard that I can barely move, but I do manage to gasp out my response.

"You all say that, right before I kill you," I say through gritted teeth.

"Hermod!" I hear Luna's voice from some distance away, and she's in trouble. It's time for me to get this situation under control.

Grunting, I reach for the changeling's throat, and take pleasure in the way the vulnerable bit of flesh in the hollow of its neck yields to the pressure of my thumbs. The creature yelps, and because it isn't expecting me to fight back in this way, I manage to toss it off me. It rolls on the ground and hits the side of the Quonset hut, while I scramble off in the direction of Luna's screams.

I chase her panicked voice through the ramshackle trailer park, and find her pinned to the ground between two homes. A changeling standing over her is pinning her shoulders down. Luna, true to form, is spewing vitriol at the creature. When this is all over, I'm going to train her to save her breath for killing demons, instead of cursing them out.

I jump on the creature's back, and hook the inside of my elbow around its neck. It is rare that I am able to catch one from this angle, and it makes it far easier to choke it out. The creature struggles ineffectually as I break its neck and wait for it to expire in my arms.

Luna rolls away and goes to her hands and knees to catch her breath. When she is finally able to speak again, the changeling is nothing more than a puddle of bubbling goo on the ground between us. I hold out my hand to help Luna to her feet.

"Did you get the other one?" she gasps. She's still short of breath and leans against me, clutching the front of my t-shirt.

"No," I tell her.

"Aren't you going to chase it down?"

"It's long gone," I say.

"They lured you here to kill you," she says. "What makes you think they won't do it again?"

"They will do it again," I say. "This isn't my first rodeo. London in 1622. East Berlin in 1987. Harlem in 1944, which was a lot of fun, by the way. Big, blond white guy fighting three changelings shifted into three little brown girls. I barely made it out of that one alive after the crowd attacked me. Good times, good times."

This elicits a spontaneous little noise from the back of her throat. She smiles and laughs. "I would have paid cash money to see you beat up three little Black girls, then run away from a crowd of angry Black people. That must have been something to see."

I frown at her, because she's still quite the brat.

We make our way through the mazes and warrens of

trailers and sheds, and soon we are standing in front of the GTO.

"Where are we going?" she asks.

"Back to my place, so I can fuck you and bite you." I tell her.

EPILOGUE

Luna

HERMOD HAS a fondness for tying me up like a Christmas turkey. Right now, I'm in the center of our bed with my face pointed to the ceiling, with my wrists and ankles tied together. He's good at tying these ropes in such a way that I don't have to use any of my muscles to maintain my position. My body is utterly slack, with just the ropes holding me in place. Large, fluffy pillows prop up my head and shoulders.

Hermod doesn't like my pussy completely bare. He prefers a longish tuft of hair on my mound, while everything else is shaved. He manages this grooming himself, using a straight razor, and does it with the reverence of a priest performing a sacred rite.

"Tell me how it went today," he says, examining my pussy carefully before planting a kiss on my clit. I tense and feel my pussy juice up under his attentions. To his right, there's a cup of foam with a shaving brush. He picks up the cup and swishes the brush around, working up the lather. I watch the glint in his eyes with fascination, waiting for the moment when he begins his ritual.

"It was fine," I say, forcing lightness into my voice. "They swore me in, I told them what I remembered, and that was pretty much that."

I flinch when Hermod begins to lather me up.

"Hold still, sweet," he says.

I let out a breath, then force myself to hold still as he painstakingly shaves me to his liking. As careful as he is, he still manages to graze one side of my pussy lips with the razor, and I hiss from the contact. When he's finished, he rolls off the bed with the shaving implements, and returns with a warm, wet towel, which feels wonderful on my cold, sensitive flesh.

I sigh. "I think you did that on purpose," I state.

"Who, me?" He cocks an eyebrow teasingly. "Why would I do that?"

"Because you like watching me bleed?" I ask.

He makes a show of removing his plush, white robe and dropping it on the floor next to the bed. I watch with avid interest as he stands before me in all his masculine glory. His body is long and muscular, lightly dusted with downy blond hairs over beautifully formed pecs and abs, and his dick is already stiff and curving towards his lower belly. My pussy is wet with anticipation. It's dripping wet, in fact, and I can feel my juices sliding toward my ass crack. My breathing becomes shallow in anticipation of what is to come.

He places a knee on the bed, then crawls over to me until he's looking up at me from between the vee of my thighs. He lowers his head to my pussy, then licks me there, along the side of my labia. His whole body shudders as he does this, and when he looks at me, licking my essence off his lips, there's a thin smear of blood on his tongue.

"Because I like kissing it better," he says. "Kissing it better, then making it worse."

He bares his needle-sharp fangs to me, then buries his face in my pussy. He's eating me urgently, sucking, licking, grazing, and when he looks up into my eyes, there are traces of my blood on his lips and chin. I'm panting, my chest heaving like a bellows, as my vampire lover eats me like the Christmas turkey I'm tied up to resemble.

I tremble as he brings me to the brink of orgasm again and again, but he won't let me finish. My throat is hoarse from my passionate screams, and I'm frustrated because my pussy is swollen and needy, and I need to release. Tears trickle from the corners of my eyes and into my ears.

"When do you go back?" he asks. He's sitting back on his haunches and looking at me, his eyes burning with lust. He trails a finger from my pussy down to my thigh, leaving a trail of blood from his bite.

"What?" I ask, confused.

"When do you have to go back?" he asks, wiping his mouth with the back of his hand.

"Um..." I say, recalling what the prosecutor told me. "They expect to have the verdict some time this week, then I'll have an opportunity to read a victim impact statement before sentencing."

"How do you feel about that?" he asks.

I don't really want to talk about this. I've never wanted to talk about this, but Hermod has a way of demanding more from me and, ultimately, it all works out, despite my discomfort in the moment.

"You have a way of forcing me to confront the things I'd rather leave in the past," I say, feeling salty. I shift against my bindings, feeling uncomfortable.

"It's because I love you," he says, shocking me.

He hasn't said any such thing since he told me he loved

me in that offhand way of his when we were doing that vampire-psychic mind meld thing when the changelings kidnapped me.

"And *this* is how you tell me?" I ask, even more cranky now. My pussy just needs a few more strokes, at the most, for me to explode like a cannon.

"I love you," he states. His cool blue eyes shimmer with passion. "I loved you the first time I met you. You were so brave, standing there ready to call the police, despite the fact you must have been scared out of your mind."

I think back on that night, just a few months ago. So much has changed since then. I can go out in daylight without feeling as though my throat is going to close up from the anxiety.

Now, thanks to Hermod, I have my life back. I have more than just my life back. I have a new purpose that I didn't have before.

"I love you too," I say, my bottom lip trembling with emotion. "Maybe not from the very beginning, but close."

"I know," he says. He's settled himself between my legs again. I'm completely helpless, but also completely safe with this man. He slides his thick, rigid cock over the lips of my pussy, which are hyper sensitive from being shaved and bitten.

He slides his thickness into me slowly, carefully. It's a tease. He's filling me inch by inch, but with very little friction, so that I cannot get off.

He grips the back of my head, holding me in place, forcing me to look deeply into his clear blue eyes.

"Say it again," he demands, his voice a low and guttural grunt. I love it when he gets this way.

"I love you," I say, shifting to capture his dick with my pussy. But the bastard only teases me.

"Again," he says. "If you want this dick, you have to tell me without reservation, sweet."

"I love you!" I scream. "I love you, I love you, I love you."

The words rip from my diaphragm in a primal scream. Nothing has ever felt this good before.

He plunges into me, hard and fast. Hard enough for my head to hit the headboard. Fast enough to make my teeth chatter.

"Again," he demands as he fucks me. He's holding me in place, pressing me into the mattress, and I'm helpless to stop him.

"I love you," I say.

He's hunched over me, his body battering mine with vicious hip jabs, muttering to himself in Old Danish, and when I'm on the edge of coming, he bites into my neck.

My pussy explodes, and tears sting and spurt behind my eyelids. I come with a yell of utter submission, baring my body, letting my soul fly apart and come together around this man as he empties himself into me.

I am a trembling mess, shaking all over, my eyelids fluttering as I come to my senses. Hermod staggers off the bed —because he, too, has been flattened by the power of our love—and heads for the bath. He returns and gives me loving aftercare, untying my ankles and wrists and rubbing them to improve the blood flow, cleaning my limbs lovingly, as I float back to earth, and my body's sexual roar settles down into a low hum.

"I have something for you," he says.

"What is it?" I ask, squinting at the metal he's holding in his hand. My eyes drift away from it to focus on his face. He's holding a heavy gold chain, which has a charm hanging from it.

"It's your collar," he says. "You will wear it, because you

belong to me, you are my heart, and I am the one meant to protect you always."

He quickly clasps the chain around my neck, and the circle charm settles into the hollow of my throat. He climbs into bed with me again, pulling me into his arms, so that my back is to his front. I finger the charm, and I make out an *H*, which has been hammered into the rough metal like a rune character.

"After you give your statement, it will be time for us to move on," he says. "Slash has found a nest of changelings in Dallas."

"Yee-haw..." I say, as I drift off to sleep in my assassin's arms.

The End

WANT MORE MIDNIGHT DOMS?

Click here to sign up for news!

Read the whole series for more of your favorite vampire BDSM club:

Alpha's Blood by Renee Rose & Lee Savino

Her Vampire Master by Maren Smith

Her Vampire Prince by Ines Johnson

Her Vampire Hero by Nicolina Martin

Her Vampire Bad Boy by Brenda Trim

Her Vampire Rebel by Zara Zenia

Her Vampire Obsession by Tymber Dalton, writing as Lesli Richardson

Her Vampire Temptation by Alexis Alvarez

Her Vampire Addiction by Tabitha Black

Her Vampire Lord by Ines Johnson

Her Vampire Suspect by Brenda Trim

His Captive Mortal by Renee Rose & Lee Savino

All Souls' Night - A Midnight Doms Anthology

The Vampire's Captive by Kay Elle Parker

The Vampire's Prey by Vivian Murdoch

ERIN ST. CHARLES

Erin grew up watching Star Trek and reading Barbara Cartland novels (don't hate), wishing she could create something that brings her love of science fiction together with her love of romance. She has a degree in journalism from Northwestern University, and an MBA from Baylor University. Still a romantic nerd at heart, she writes sensual, diverse stories that blend fantasy, adventure, and love.

www.erinstcharles.com

Join the Erin St. Charles newsletter for updates and receive a FREE novella, CLOSE ENOUGH TO LOVE: https://erinstcharles.com/newsletter/

ALSO BY ERIN ST. CHARLES

Contemporary Romance

A KISS TO THE RESCUE — Richard and Keisha

SLEIGH MY NAME — Tor and Holly

TOUGH CUSTOMER — Lincoln and Samantha

Paranormal Romance

THAT TIME SHE BROKE HER VIKING'S CURSE — Auntie and
Gunnar

THE MINOTAUR'S KISS — Shifter Enforcers Book One: Mac and
Diana

THE WOLF'S CONCUBINE — Shifter Enforcers Book Two:
Phelan and Lola

THE WOLF'S SUCCUBUS — Shifter Enforcers Book Three: Eric
and Jane

THE ALPHA TAKES A BRIDE — Shifter Enforcers Book Four:
Bubba and Vanessa

THE MINOTAUR NEXT DOOR – Shifter Enforcers Book Five:
Blake and Sophia

Printed in Great Britain
by Amazon

56321828R00119